To Fran,

A Summer
in Peach Creek

Michele Malo

Michele Malo

Beagle Bay Press

First print edition: December 2014
ISBN-13: 978-1505555417
ISBN-10: 1505555418

Published by Beagle Bay Press
http://www.michelemalo.com/
Contact: michelemaloauthor@gmail.com

Cover art by Nancy Stanchfield and Temre Stanchfield
Graphic design by Willo Bellwood
Interior design by Annie Pearson

Newspaper headlines are quoted or derived from *The Secret Life and Brutal Death of Mamie Thurman*, by F. Keith Davis, copyright 2001, and from the archives of the *Logan Banner*.

To J.O. Ward
who told the stories

A SUMMER IN PEACH CREEK

PROLOGUE

SUMMERS IN SEATTLE NEVER FELT LIKE THIS, Faith thought. Drops of sweat trickled down between her ample breasts and made dark stains on her blue cotton blouse. She still couldn't get over the heat and the humidity even though she had been here all summer. Faith wiped the back of her neck with a handkerchief that Mama had embroidered with lilies of the valley and a fancy "F" in the corner for her seventeenth birthday last November. For just a moment Faith was transported from Logan, West Virginia, back home to the Pacific Northwest. Faith closed her eyes tightly and conjured up the cool marine air as it drifted up the hill from Elliott Bay.

"How much longer do you think, Papa, before the verdict comes?" asked Faith. "My feet hurt and my hair is a frizzled mess." She had been standing on the courthouse steps since one o'clock waiting for Bart Strout from the *Logan Tribune* to come out with the verdict from the trial. It was almost three and not a word. Her cousin Nell was with her, rattling on, as usual, about what she was going to wear to Faith's going-away party tonight. Faith's father, Charles, was in front of her, just a step below. Faith fingered the new charm bracelet on her wrist with its single charm—a sterling silver peach with 1932

1

engraved on the leaf. Henry had given it to her the night before. Nell was still discussing what they should wear tonight when Faith noticed the beanpole of a reporter, holding a pencil and a notepad, step up on a wooden apple crate.

"Shhh," said Faith to Nell. "Here comes Bart. I think he's got the verdict."

The crowd of nearly a thousand stood shoulder to shoulder on the marble steps and the yard below, peering over the folks in front to get a glimpse of the reporter.

"Quiet, everyone," shouted Bart. "We've got a verdict."

Faith put her hands behind her back and crossed her fingers.

Not guilty, not guilty, she wished.

The crowd fell silent.

PART ONE

JUNE, 1932
THE MURDER

MAIN STREET IN THE SMALL town of Peach Creek was appropriately lined with peach trees. The peaches hung thick on the trees like clusters of green marbles. They held a promise of late-summer pies and cobblers and jams.

ONE

FAITH WOKE UP BEFORE NELL. She tried to go back to sleep but the windows were open, and between the crickets chirping, the bullfrogs croaking, and the birds singing and calling, it was hopeless. Besides, she was sweating and the sheets were damp. It was already so humid it felt as if you could wring out the air. Faith crept out of her side of the bed, pulled on her robe, and tiptoed down the stairs, being careful not to wake up her cousin Nell. They had stayed up past midnight talking. Nell had given her a rundown of all the popular boys at school. A boy named Henry Thompson was at the top of the list: captain of the football team and the most handsome boy in Logan, at least according to Nell.

It's like I've known Nell my whole life, almost like we're sisters, thought Faith. *Papa always said that blood was thicker than water. I think I get it now. There's something, some kind of invisible connection, that's so different from my friendships back home.*

Faith went out on the front porch that stretched the full length of the Cole house. She found her father reading the paper in an old wooden rocker upholstered in a cracked dark-brown leather. Faith pulled up the wicker rocker next to him.

"Good morning, Sweet Pea. I'm not used to you getting up with the chickens."

"Hi, Papa."

"Have trouble sleeping in this heat, or are you just too excited to stay in bed?"

"A little of both, I guess. I can hardly believe we're finally here," said Faith.

As if on cue, Aunt Kitty poked her head out and handed them each a steaming cup of coffee. "I'm going to start breakfast pretty soon, but I'll let Sis and the children sleep a little longer. We were all up later than usual last night. I had to pinch myself this morning 'cause I still can't believe you're all here. I wasn't sure you'd ever come. How'd you sleep?"

"Just fine," Papa responded.

"Me, too. Thanks for the coffee, Aunt Kitty. Do you want some help?"

"No, this is your first morning in Peach Creek. You just enjoy the birds this morning."

Aunt Kitty went back inside.

Faith settled in on the wide front porch of the big house on Main Street. She looked across the small yard enclosed with a wire fence. The fence was covered in morning glories, the same bright blue as the Cole's house. Today was just the beginning, the first day of her family's summerlong visit. There were so many relatives to meet and so much to learn about this corner of West Virginia with its mountain roads, clear streams, hills, and hollers.

Faith took a big gulp of her coffee and winced. She looked over at her father. He laughed.

"I'm with you, Faith. It's pretty bad, about as strong as old dishwater."

Her coffee wasn't great, but Aunt Kitty outdid herself with a big country breakfast. There were biscuits and gravy, ham steaks, and fried eggs from the chickens that lived out back. Faith was used to the coffee at Broadway Lunch in Seattle, which her family had owned and run for the last six years. The coffee back home was rich and strong. She looked at Papa across the table as they both took a sip. Papa winked at her, but neither said a word. After breakfast, Faith dressed in a pale-yellow cotton dress with cap sleeves and rickrack trim that she had made back home.

"We need to leave for church in ten minutes," said Uncle George.

Faith rode with Nell and the Coles to Logan First Baptist Church. Logan was the county seat and the biggest town around, just four miles from Peach Creek. Papa drove the old pickup. He dropped Faith's mom, Sadie, and nine-year-old sister, Marion, off in front of the redbrick church where they met up with the rest of the family. He promised to pick them up at noon.

Faith's father wasn't the church-going type. He liked to remind anyone within earshot that the only reason he went to Sunday school as a boy was because Sadie was the teacher. When they got married, he figured that was the Lord's way of giving him permission to stay home on Sundays. After all, he was living with a Sunday-school teacher twenty-four hours a day, seven days a week, and she did enough praying for the both of them. Sadie never argued with him about it. Faith knew that the reason her mother didn't want the story told was because it was then evident that Sadie was older than her husband. Five years, to be exact, as Marion was apt to pronounce once she was old enough to do the math.

The preacher, Reverend Corn, was bombastic, pounding on the lectern as his big voice rose, calling on his parishioners to live their faith and not be hypocrites. Despite the preacher's booming rhetoric, Faith's mind drifted to the swim party planned for this afternoon. It would be so nice to dip in the cool river, but having everyone see her in her bathing suit was unnerving.

Faith's whole body flinched as the organ cranked up, and the choir, in matching purple robes, began to sing "Nearer, My God, to Thee." The hymn was the same as the one that Faith sang at the New Baptist Church in Seattle. Her voice was clear and strong. She loved to sing and knew all the words by heart. Right after the opening song, the preacher asked newcomers to stand and introduce themselves. When Sadie, Marion, and Faith stood, everyone burst into applause. *They all remember Mama,* Faith thought. It was clear that the church members were very happy to see that Sadie had returned to her childhood church.

"There's Henry's family," whispered Nell, poking Faith with her elbow. The five Thompsons were seated right up front, Mr. Thompson in a fine pin-striped suit and Mrs. Thompson in a smart gray linen dress. The two little girls had matching white bows holding back golden ringlets. They looked like twins. Henry was wearing a simple gray light-weight suit with a white-and-green-striped tie. He sat tall in the pew.

He looks sharp, thought Faith. *Shoot, why am I even looking at him?*

Even though Nell had assured Faith that there was nothing between her and Henry, Faith was pretty sure Nell would love to be his girlfriend.

A boy like that would never be interested in me; besides Nell has her eye on him, Faith thought.

Henry's family left right after church before Nell could catch up and introduce Faith.

"You're so right, Nell. He really is dreamy," said Faith. And he was.

"Don't worry, Faith. We'll see Henry at the Mill. I'll introduce you there."

Home from church, Sadie, Kitty, Nell, and Faith donned aprons and began to put the picnic together. Sadie got the chicken out of the ice chest where it had been soaking overnight in buttermilk. She dredged it in seasoned flour and slid the pieces into the hot lard in a huge cast-iron frying pan.

"You could knock me over with a feather," said Kitty, putting her arm around Sadie's shoulder. "I still can't believe you're here, Sis. It's like you never left. You haven't changed one little bit."

Faith knew this wasn't true. Her mother's hair had gray streaks and wrinkles lined her forehead.

Aunt Kitty was vibrant and fresh. Her blue eyes sparkled and her ready smile was warm. Kitty had red hair just like Faith's—just as unruly as hers—but on Kitty it created a warm halo around her happy face.

Mama looks older than Aunt Kitty and she's at least two years younger.

"And look at you girls! Spin around and let me take a long look at the two of you again," said their aunt. "You're beautiful."

Marion beamed.

With that Kitty chopped the sweet pickles, green onions, and celery and added them to her famous potato salad. She stirred in the mayonnaise and mustard and the sweet pickle juice from the jar, all the while tasting small spoonsful to get the seasoning just right. Finally she chopped up half a dozen hard-boiled eggs and gently folded them in.

"You make it just like Mama taught me," said Faith to her aunt.

"Old family recipe," replied Kitty with a smile. "You're either a sweet pickle or a dill family; we're sweet."

Faith and Nell were in charge of slicing the pound cake and washing the strawberries that Marion and Rusty had picked from the patch out back before church. They also squeezed the lemons and made a big jar of lemonade and one of sweet tea.

Faith watched her mother with wonder. Sadie was laughing as she fried the chicken. It was a rare treat to hear that bell-like laugh. She seemed more relaxed in this big boisterous kitchen, flour flying, brushing back wayward strands of hair with the back of her hand, than she ever did back home in their apartment kitchen with its small electric stove. In fact, Sadie was rarely in that little kitchen, since she spent most of the day behind their lunch counter on Broadway. By the time she plopped down on the couch at home, the last thing she wanted to think about was cooking more food. So Faith, Marion, and Charles took most of their meals at the lunch counter. The feeling in the Cole kitchen was such a contrast. It was loud, a little chaotic, and full of laughter.

When everything was ready, Kitty packed the picnic food into a big wicker basket, and the jars of lemonade and sweet tea were set in a bucket of ice that sat in Rusty's beat-up red wagon. Peck's Landing was a short hike, mostly uphill, on the old mining road. It was still hot, but the soggy clouds had cleared and the air felt warm and fresh on Faith's skin.

"You'll love the Mill," said Nell. "There's a covered picnic area and they even have a place to change into our swimsuits. I'm dying, it's been hotter than a pistol all week. Oh, goodness, do you know how to swim? I forgot to ask."

Faith had to concentrate to keep up. Nell was a whirlwind, hardly taking a breath when she talked, which seemed to Faith to be all the time. But Faith already liked her. Nell had a way about her that made a person feel right at home. It was a relief after all those weeks of worrying about whether she would fit in with her cousin. She hoped Nell's friends would be as easy to get to know.

They were the last to arrive at the swimming hole. "I'll never be able to remember all these names," said Faith.

"Give yourself some time," said Uncle George. "You've got all summer."

There was one name Faith had no trouble remembering—Henry Thompson. Henry was even more handsome up close. His lanky arms and legs were all browned up, his sandy hair hung low over his eyebrows, and his clear blue eyes were directed straight at Faith.

"Nice to meet you. Nell hasn't stopped talking about you since she heard you all were coming," he said, shaking her hand. "But then she hardly ever stops talking," he gave Nell a little laugh and a wink.

"Shame on you, Henry Thompson," said Nell, her whole face lighting up as she flipped her long black hair back.

Faith was taken aback with Henry's ease and handsome charm. Soon all the teenagers were settled on blankets near the river's edge, plates piled high with picnic food.

"Sit here, Faith," said Henry, as he motioned to a spot on a faded quilt next to him.

Caught off guard by Henry's attention, Faith followed his invitation. Before she was completely settled, Nell motioned to her. "Move over, cousin." She sat down between Faith and Henry and immediately began talking so fast that Faith could barely answer the questions that came her way from the teenagers seated around her.

"What's it like out West? Do you have real Indians? Does it snow all the time?" In truth, Seattle was more sophisticated than Peach Creek and far bigger, but Faith didn't say so. Mostly she felt a little uncomfortable being the center of all this attention.

Lunch over, the girls went to the shed by the river to change into swimsuits. The boys just stripped off their trousers and jumped in the mountain stream.

"Come on in," they shouted, as the girls came out.

There was no way to hide her curvy figure. Faith wrapped her large breasts and hips in a towel hoping no one would notice, then dropped the towel at the riverbank and ran into the deep pool of water as fast as she could. Faith had been self-conscious ever since Tommy Carlson had teased her in fifth grade when she was the first girl in her class to develop.

Faith watched as Nell and her friends waded in slowly, squealing as the chilly water crept up their ankles, all in a successful bid to have the boys look at them. Nell's legs went on forever. She was a good head taller than Faith, with porcelain skin and coal-black hair that hung straight to her shoulders. It caught the light like polished onyx.

If I just had Nell's legs to go along with my big bust and that hair of hers, I'd be a bomb shell, Faith laughed to herself.

"Are you doing OK, Faith?" asked Henry, taking his eyes off the rest of the girls as they inched themselves into the icy stream. "It's awful cold water, from the snow runoff. By August the temperature is just about perfect, but it's only June."

"I'm used to swimming in Puget Sound. It's just as cold. Papa says you'd never get in if you didn't just jump in. It doesn't take long before you just go numb."

Henry laughed a laugh that started with his eyes crinkling up and his nose making a little snorting sound. Finally his whole body took over. Faith felt goose bumps and it wasn't just from the cold water.

No one stayed in the water long. It really was too cold to swim for more than a few minutes. In fact, the other girls only managed to get in up to their knees.

"That girl's got guts," Henry said to no one in particular.

The next week the Dansworth family was carted in all directions for introductions to more relatives and neighbors. Faith felt overwhelmed. There was a quilting bee, a Bible study class where Faith played the piano for the preacher, a trip to Logan to see a movie, and many late nights when Faith and Nell chatted and swooned over all the dreamy boys in Peach Creek and Logan. Henry Thompson was always the favorite topic.

Late on Saturday afternoon, Sadie and Kitty went over to their sister-in-law Margaret's house down Main Street to join the sewing circle who were crocheting baby blankets for the missions in China. Papa and Uncle George were up at the top of the mining road sawing fallen trees and chopping the logs to stockpile wood for the winter. That left Nell and Faith in charge of Rusty and Marion.

"Why don't you and Marion go over to the creek and see who can throw rocks the farthest?" said Nell to her little brother, not quite a year older than Marion who was nine.

"Please, don't just hang around us, Marion. Find something to do. Go play," said Faith, annoyed to once again be left in charge of Marion.

Rusty looked at Marion dressed in bloomers and a flour-sack dress that Mama insisted she wear when she played outdoors.

"There's no point in ruining a perfectly good outfit when I know you're going to dig in the dirt or find a puddle to splash in," Sadie would say.

Rusty dismissed his cousin with a look that Marion did not accept.

"Girls don't know how to throw."

"Let's just find out about that, Rusty Cole," said Marion, hand on hips.

The gauntlet was thrown as Marion and Rusty raced each other across the street to the creek bank. Peach Creek was running fast over the rocks, no more than fifteen feet wide in most places.

Faith turned to Nell. "Poor Rusty. He doesn't know what he's in for."

The girls watched as Marion beat her cousin to the bank and began heaving rocks across the little stream.

Faith and Nell laughed as they sewed lace to the hems of the matching skirts they had made earlier that week. They were planning to wear their new skirts to Sunday school the next day. Both were hoping Henry would be at church but hadn't told each other.

"Do you want some iced tea? I'll slice us a piece of pound cake, too. I'm so hot I could die," said Nell. "You'd think I'd get used to the heat. Golly, I hate to sweat."

Nell got up before Faith had a chance to answer and went inside to pour the tea. The cousins had been so engrossed in their sewing that Faith had lost track of time, so she was somewhat surprised when she looked up to see Rusty crossing the road alone.

"Where's Marion, Rusty?" shouted Faith.

"I dunno. She said she wanted to go look for frogs. Last I saw her she was heading upstream along the bank."

Nell came through the door with their tea.

Faith looked at Nell.

"Marion went off without checking with me. I'd better go after her. Mother'll kill me if she finds out Marion's wandered off by herself."

Faith dumped her skirt and the trim back in the sewing basket and took off across the road and up Peach Creek.

"Wait for me," called Nell to Faith. "Rusty, you stay put, and I mean it. Do not leave this house in case Marion gets back before we do. I can't believe you let that girl go off by herself when she doesn't know a thing about the hills around these parts."

Nell caught up with Faith. They called Marion's name as they went along the stream bank.

"Where did she run off to? I'm gonna kill her," said Faith.

Faith found a long stick and poked under ferns and bushes.

"Maybe she fell in the water." said Faith.

"Not hardly," said Nell. "The creek's pretty shallow in most spots, even though the snow runoff is awfully heavy. We'll find her."

Faith thought of all the copperhead stories Papa had told, especially the one where the snake had bitten his heel when he was a boy in this very stream, and how his pa had cut a slit in the bite, sucked out the blood, then plunged his foot in a coffee can of tobacco spit and held it there for an hour. Papa even had the scar to prove it. Faith's mind began to spin.

"What if Marion's lying under a rhododendron bush dying of a snakebite?"

Tears started to leak out of Faith's eyes as she scoured the creek bank. The girls had followed the creek up the hill for about a mile with no sign of Marion.

"Let's cross over to the other side of the creek and work our way back," said Nell.

The brush was thicker, and it took longer to check the underbrush and look behind rocks, but Faith and Nell kept at it. The longer they were out, the more scared Faith became. Faith could tell that Nell was worried, too, but was trying to be calm so Faith wouldn't panic.

It's not that Mama will be furious, which she will, Faith thought. *It's that the thought of anything happening to my baby sister is just too much to bear.*

Nell put her arm across Faith's shoulder as they reached the spot where Rusty and Marion had been playing directly across from the house. The cousins crossed the street to the Cole home without Marion. Now Faith's hope was that Marion had found her way back home by herself.

"She's used to playing alone in our apartment when Mama, Papa, and I are working at the lunch counter. She just walks the two blocks to the store when she gets bored or hungry. There's never been a problem," said Faith to Nell. "Besides, she is a true tomboy and loves to be outdoors. I bet she just lost track of time." She said this more to reassure herself than to inform Nell.

Before she reached the top stair of the porch, Faith knew Marion hadn't come back. Papa and Uncle George were standing there, their work clothes covered with sawdust.

"How long have you been gone?" asked Papa. "George and I are going out in the truck. He knows the woods real well. We'll find Peanut. Don't you worry."

Faith looked at him, and now the tears came in buckets.

"It's all my fault. I wasn't paying attention. Nell and I were having so much fun working on our skirts and talking that I didn't even look across the road. What if Marion . . ."

"Stop that, Faith. Marion can take care of herself. She's probably captured a poor unsuspecting frog and has already named him and has him in her pocket and is heading for home," Papa said.

With that, he and Uncle George climbed into the battered truck still loaded with firewood and headed up the mountain road. Nell and Rusty decided to look along the banks downstream even though Rusty insisted that Marion had taken off the other way.

Nell looked her little brother in the eye and said, "You should never have let her go up the creek by herself. She hasn't been here a week and she doesn't know her way around these parts."

Faith waited at home alone in case her sister showed up. Faith could hear Nell and Rusty in the distance shouting Marion's name as she said a prayer. It was all she could think to do. *Dear Jesus, please bring Marion home safe. She's not the one who should suffer. Let it be me. I have been selfish and mean. If you need to punish someone, let it be me*, Faith prayed to herself.

An hour went by, Nell and her brother were long ago out of sight, and the men hadn't returned. Faith felt helpless as she paced across the big covered front porch. Then, Faith heard footsteps on the gravel. At the foot of the stairs stood Marion. She wasn't alone. Holding her hand was a young colored man, and beside him were three lean beagles sniffing around the bushes. Faith was so startled she just stared at the sight of them for a second. Marion looked fine except for swollen eyes and tearstained cheeks. Her flour-sack dress was covered in mud.

The fellow with the dogs was short for a grown man, dressed in gray overalls and work boots. A gray-and-white striped railroad hat covered most of his short-cropped black hair. His skin was dark and shiny. What she noticed most were his hands. He was missing both of his pinky fingers.

"Marion! Where have you been? We've all been scared spitless. Papa, Uncle George, Nell, and Rusty are all out looking for you. I hiked at least a mile up Peach Creek looking for you."

Faith rushed down the stairs and caught Marion up in her arms. "Oh, thank goodness you're home safe." The sisters held each other tight and began blubbering together.

"It's all right, Peanut. It's all right. Don't you worry. No one's mad at you."

"Oh, Sis," Marion spoke between sobs. "I was just looking for frogs, and then I got all turned around and started walking in the wrong direction, I guess. I was so afraid."

"It's my fault. I should have been paying more attention to you. It's my fault. Do you forgive me?" Faith implored.

Then she realized the young man standing beside them had stepped a few feet back as if to give them space and a degree of privacy.

"I'm so sorry. How rude of me. My name is Faith Dansworth and this is my little sister, Marion." She held out her hand. "We're from Washington State so I'm not surprised Marion got lost. You must have found her. How can I ever thank you?"

The man looked at his feet. He seemed embarrassed as he timidly shook Faith's hand. Finally he spoke in the softest drawl. Faith had to strain to hear his voice.

"How do. I'm Sidney Williams but folks call me Pinky. I was out with the dogs when I heard someone whimpering."

At this point Faith looked at the three dogs now rolling on their backs in the dirt.

He continued. "I found this child a couple of yards away crying and holdin' on to the fattest frog I've ever seen. I figured she was lost. I asked her where she lived. She told me she was staying at the Cole place in Peach Creek."

"And I still got the frog, Faith," interrupted Marion.

Both Faith and Sidney burst out laughing as Marion held up the poor creature that had been hiding in her pocket, just as Papa had predicted.

"And I suppose you've named him, too?" said Faith.

"Yep. I'm calling him Broadway after our store."

Faith invited Sidney to come up on the porch and have a glass of iced tea and some pound cake.

"Thanks, Miss, but I need to get the dogs back to Logan, and I've got to pick up my mail at the post office here," he replied, eyes still looking at the ground.

Faith insisted that he take the pound cake with him.

"It's the least I can do. My goodness, you rescued Marion and brought her home to us. I wish there was more I could do to thank you," Faith said.

She went to the kitchen and wrapped up the rest of the pound cake in waxed paper, came back out and handed the package to Sidney who was still standing at the foot of the stairs. He took it and was turning to leave when Marion reached up and kissed him on the cheek before he knew what was happening. He seemed startled by her little kiss but smiled a smile that reached from one ear to the other. He tucked the cake under his arm and whistled for the dogs who had run off down by the creek. Sidney then tipped his hat to the girls. Marion and Faith, holding hands, watched as he and the three dogs headed south down Main Street toward the post office.

Everyone returned home at once. Faith and Marion and Rusty each had a version of the story to tell. Mother and Aunt Kitty were mesmerized and the household burst into laughter when Marion pulled the poor old frog from her pocket again.

"I think that fellow might like a bug and some water," said Uncle George.

"And I've got a shoe box that would make a fine home if you filled it with some grass," said Aunt Kitty.

Rusty and Marion spent the next thirty minutes fixing a home for Broadway and hunting him up some dinner.

"I don't know why Sidney didn't want to eat pound cake with us," said Marion.

"Lordy, Marion. He's colored," said Nell, rolling her eyes. *What's that all about?* thought Faith.

"I know you're segregated here, but I didn't think it meant coloreds and whites couldn't eat a piece of pound cake together. Mr. Johnson, he's colored, and he works at Broadway lunch. He and Papa drink beer and play cards in the dining room after work now and then."

Papa and Uncle George went out to unload and stack the firewood from the pickup, and Kitty went in to start supper, which left Faith alone in the parlor with her mother.

Well, here it comes.

To her surprise, Mother was quite gentle with her.

"Faith, I am proud of how you handled all of this. It's just like your sis to go off looking for some critter without thinking. I hope she's learned her lesson about walking off into unknown parts. She will sleep like a lamb tonight, that's for sure."

Faith replied, "It wasn't Marion's fault. I was too busy talking with Nell. I should have been paying closer attention. I'm sorry, Mama. From now on I promise I'll keep a better eye on her."

"You did just fine, honey. You're not to blame."

Sadie gave Faith a sideways little hug and a kiss on the top of her head, just like she used to when Faith was little, and then Sadie went to the kitchen to help her sister. Faith stood there shocked and relieved.

TWO

LATER THAT EVENING, THE GROWN-UPS settled on the porch as the moon rose. The air was sweet with honeysuckle and the moon was full. The children were all asleep, even Faith and Nell. Marion's disappearance had taken the starch out of everyone. Charles had many questions about the day, mostly concerning Marion's rescuer, Sidney Williams: who was he and what was he doing in Peach Creek? Did they have anything to worry about when it came to the children?

"Sidney Williams is a regular around these parts. He's got a sister in Logan, Precious Williams, who takes in laundry and is also a fine midwife." George took a sip of coffee and continued. "He was brought up here from Mississippi with a bunch of coloreds by the mine owners who thought they wouldn't go union. Sidney settled in Peach Creek down by the Front, lived here for about six or seven years, I think. He used to work up at the Peach Creek Mine handling the mules. He'd had lots of experience with those animals when he was sharecropping in Mississippi. Some say Sidney has a special gift with animals."

"Why do they call him Pinky?" asked Sadie.

"Poor fella lost his pinky fingers in two separate accidents at the mine. Both times his finger got caught in the chains as they were loading up and moving out the coal cars. It's a pity 'cause he's a scrappy little fellow. Everyone likes him. He works like a mule himself, amazingly strong for being such a small man," said George.

"I'm so grateful to him for finding Marion. She could still be out there alone in the night if it weren't for him." Sadie shuddered for a moment, so Charles put his arm around her shoulders. "Wish there was something more we could do. Where does he live now?" asked Sadie.

Kitty chimed in, "I heard he's living at the Thompsons' in Logan. Mrs. Thompson mentioned something at Women's League about her husband taking him in as a handyman when Precious told them he was out of work and had fallen on hard times. Apparently, Precious does their laundry. Hazel Thompson hardly has to lift a finger. She's got a housekeeper and a cook. I guess that frees her up to go golfing at the country club. Must be nice."

"Now, Kitty," said her husband, "Hazel Thompson's a good Christian woman just like yourself."

Kitty rolled her eyes just as her daughter had earlier, but she did stop talking. Charles and George took out cigars, bit off the tips and lit them.

"We're going to Hazel's house for Women's League on Monday. You can see for yourself."

"What does her husband do?" asked Sadie.

"He works at Logan First National Bank. He's also an elder at church and president of the city council. Quite the bigwig. I heard he's a drinker."

"Kitty," said Sadie, giving her sister a withering look.

"Well, it's true. Isn't it, George?" asked Kitty.

The conversation waned because everyone else refused to feed it. Charles hated gossip and started talking about the upcoming fight in Chicago. Sadie brought out her embroidery, and Kitty began knitting. The two couples spent another hour content, until Kitty tiptoed into new territory.

"I'm glad that you didn't fly off the handle with Faith this afternoon, but I am upset that Nell wasn't watching the children like she shoulda been, and I gave Rusty a dressing down for letting Marion go up the creek without him. You did the right thing, though. I think Faith has punished herself enough. Besides, all's well that ends well."

Charles cocked an ear toward the women's conversation and said, "It's good that you went easy on Faith. We expect too much from her."

"I know. I surprised myself. There's no question I demand a lot from Faith. She works at the lunch counter and she watches over her sister, too. And hardly ever complains." Sadie sighed. "Being back here has caused me to see things fresh. I don't know. I've been so tired for so long. Losing Becky was hard on us all, but her passing brought me to my knees."

Rarely did Sadie say so much. Charles was surprised that his wife was talking about the baby. George raised his eyebrows.

"Maybe it would be good for you to visit your Mama and Becky's graves while you are here," said George.

"I don't know if I can."

THREE

THE FOLLOWING MONDAY, THE TEMPERATURE rose and the humidity matched it by nine in the morning. It was so hot that Aunt Kitty let everyone skip the morning chores.

"What we need is a good ole-fashioned gully washer to wring these clouds out. Just leave the dishes in the sink. They're not going anywhere and maybe by supper it will have cooled down a bit," said Kitty, wiping the back of her neck with a damp dish towel.

Faith was dumbstruck. Mother would never leave dishes in the sink. *Why can't Mama be more like Aunt Kitty?*

Kitty continued, "You girls better skedaddle and finish getting dressed. Sadie and I are leaving for Logan in thirty minutes and we're not waiting on the two of you. Our league meeting starts at eleven sharp. We'll be there for lunch, so you girls can pick out your fabric at Rhodes and then go to Leonetti's for lunch."

Logan, the county seat, was more than twice the size of Peach Creek, bustling most days with shoppers and office workers. The Logan First National Bank, which sat on the corner of First and Main, was imposing with its granite facade. The courthouse with its elegant white columns stood guard in front of the main square. Almost all the other downtown buildings were made of red- or cream-colored brick from the local clay sources. Down a block from the bank, the Acamada Hotel stood three stories tall. There were two department stores and the offices for the *Logan Tribune*, the regional newspaper. Numerous lunch counters, restaurants, and bakeries dotted the streets, many of them run by Italian families who had settled here in hopes of landing mining jobs. Two boarding houses stood near Harris Funeral Home on the banks of the Guyandotte River.

Kitty dropped the girls off at Rhodes Mercantile, right across the street from the bank.

"We should be done by two, so please be at the Thompsons' on time. No dawdling," said Kitty.

The cousins went straight to the bolts of voile fabric. They had patterns for elaborate dresses to wear to Aunt Elizabeth's fete next month, and the gauzy voile would be perfect.

"Pick the yellow, Faith. It will show off your red hair to its best advantage. I think this eggshell pink will look perfect against my skin. I've been careful to cover up in the sun so I'm not all covered in freckles. Oops! Sorry, Faith. I love your freckles. You are a spittin' image of your mama and my mama. You can spot a Hackworth a mile off with their red hair and freckles. I'm the only one who got my daddy's coloring. It's the black Irish, he says, that gave us the dark hair and porcelain complexion. Even Rusty . . ."

"Shhh. Look across the street. Isn't that Henry Thompson going into the bank?"

Nell poked her head between the bolts of fabric.

"Oh, gosh, it is! Hurry up. Maybe we can pretend to run into him when he comes out. He's probably at the bank to see his father."

Faith wasn't sure about this plan of Nell's, but Nell was already moving toward the door. Nell dropped her bolt of pink voile on the counter and told the clerk they would be back after lunch to pick out eyelet, thread, and buttons. Faith followed with the yellow bolt.

As casually as the girls could manage, they strolled across the street, lingering at the front window of McDonald's Department Store as if mesmerized by the display of sundresses and hats. It wasn't long before Henry pushed through the heavy swinging bank doors backwards, his arms weighted down with official-looking folders. Nell planted herself smack in front of his backside. He didn't see her, turned, bumped into her, and proceeded to drop the entire pile.

"Oh, I'm so sorry, Henry, I didn't see you coming out. Here, let me help you pick these up," said Nell, flashing a flirty smile. "Goodness, they've flown everywhere."

"That's OK, I should have been paying more attention," said Henry.

He looked down and almost stumbled over Faith. She was already on her knees, gathering files and loose papers with no idea what belonged where.

I wish I could disappear. This is so obvious, Faith thought.

"How are we ever going to get this stuff back in its proper order?" asked Faith.

Henry knelt down and assured her that it wasn't as difficult as it might seem.

"Each file has a code number at the top and all the papers match the file code."

Faith handed him a stack of papers. Their hands touched briefly, and Faith felt the heat rise from her neck to her ears.

Egads, I'm sure every freckle on my face is lit up, she thought.

Henry smiled and looked directly at her ears which she was sure had turned crimson.

"Why, thank you, Miss Faith. You are awfully kind to help, but it's much too hot and muggy for you and Nell to be kneeling on this pavement. You could fry an egg on it."

"Nonsense, Henry Thompson. We're at your service," said Nell. "Would you like to join us for lunch at Leonetti's when we're done?"

Faith cringed.

"Thanks, but I have to deliver this stuff to the bank's attorney. His office is a few blocks away, and then I'm meeting some of the guys to run track."

Faith stood up, straightened her skirt, and pulled her hair back from her face, tucking the loose strands that were always escaping back under the ribbon.

"You be careful. You can get heat exhaustion in this weather," said Faith.

"Why, thank you, Faith. I didn't know you cared," said Henry.

He winked and tossed her a smile over his shoulder as he sprinted down the street. She could feel her ears heating up again. Nell gave Faith a withering look as they headed for lunch.

Few words were spoken at lunch, but as they were sipping the last of their pineapple sodas, Nell blurted out, "I hope you know that Henry is just being nice to you because you are my guest for the summer. He's nice to everyone. I wouldn't expect that he'll fall for you, if that's what you are thinking."

"Who said I expect him to fall for me?"

After lunch the cousins went back to the store to purchase their fabric and notions. They each bought four yards of fabric for their dresses. The pattern called for a very full skirt and an eyelet petticoat. The bodice had tiny vertical pleats with little pearl buttons down the front. It was a big undertaking and would take several weeks to complete, especially if they added the French knot trim around the neckline. But it would be worth it. Nell's Aunt Elizabeth was planning a fortieth birthday party for Aunt Kitty.

"There'll even be a live band and dancing," Nell told her.

"Are you ready?" asked Faith. "We need to hurry or we'll be late for our ride."

"I'm coming. You don't need to get all riled up," said Nell.

"I'll wait for you outside," said Faith, clenching her hands tightly.

She stood on the sidewalk waiting for Nell, knowing they were going to be late. Faith's mouth was dry, so she walked a few steps to a drinking fountain on the corner. A little Negro girl, no more than four, her head bobbing with a thousand neat little braids, was trying to reach the spout. Faith went to her.

"Here, let me help."

She reached down and lifted the child up to the spout while she turned the faucet on. Out of nowhere a Negro woman yanked the girl from Faith's arm and slapped the little girl on her backside.

"Don't you ever let me catch you doin' that again," she yelled as she turned, the child still clutched under her arm, and disappeared around the corner. During the brief episode the woman never looked at Nell or said a word to her. Faith felt a tightening in her belly.

"What was all that commotion?" asked Nell as she flew through the store's double doors.

"I was just helping a little girl get a drink . . ."

"Was she a Negro child?"

"Yes, but . . ."

Nell interrupted Faith and pointed to a white sign with bold black letters: Whites Only.

"Good lord, Faith."

Faith didn't utter a single word on the ride home. She stared out the window and hugged her side of the back seat. Chores were done in silence. The rains never came. The family ate cold cuts and cottage cheese and sliced tomatoes from Kitty's garden for supper and everyone slept on top of the covers. Faith drifted off thinking of the wink, the touch, and the smile. And the little girl with the thousand braids.

Faith woke at dawn to lightning flashing through the open windows. The curtains were flapping and the thunder was so powerful that it shook the books off the nightstand. At breakfast the main topic was the summer storm.

"Marion crawled in between us," said Papa. "She got frightened by the thunder."

"I did not! I was cold, that's all," said Marion.

"Yea, right," said Rusty.

Four and a half inches of rain fell, breaking all records. It rained so hard that the Methodist church across the road was covered in fifteen inches of mud from Peach Creek.

"I can't ever remember that little creek overflowing and I've lived here my whole life," said Kitty.

With the heavy rains the air finally cooled, so Sadie and Kitty took advantage of the drop in temperature and baked pies. Marion and Rusty amused themselves with games of cowboys and Indians in the dining room, making tents and forts out of old quilts. Nell and Faith began to work on their elaborate party dresses. The ice between them began to thaw as they pinned and cut the patterns and measured each other.

"Hey, watch it there, Missy," said Faith, as Nell stretched the measuring tape around Faith's big bust.

"I can't help it, Faith. You've got a lot to measure," giggled Nell.

Faith tried to hold her laughter in, but it was impossible.

"Please don't be mad at me, Nell, just because Henry winked at me. It doesn't mean anything. He likes you," said Faith.

"I don't think so," said Nell with a sigh.

We really are kindred spirits, Faith thought. *We may not look like we are related but it feels like she could be my sister.*

When George got home from his railroad job at the Front, the conversation shifted from the big rain to the fight of the week.

"Tonight's the big boxing match in Chicago, between Schmeling and Sharkey," said George.

"My money's on Schmeling," said Charles.

"We should listen to the match at Randy's Roadhouse. It's on the outskirts of Logan," said George. "All the fellows will be there."

"I thought the fight didn't start till eight. It's only six," said Kitty.

Faith watched her papa and Uncle George push away from the table as soon as they wolfed down their supper. They kissed their wives and started out the back door.

"The place'll be packed. We want to get a table close to the radio. It's going to be hard to hear otherwise," said George.

"Can I come, too?" asked Rusty.

"Sure. In about ten years," laughed his Uncle Charles.

Sadie laughed and called to the men as they headed out the door, "You could stay home and listen right here. You know there's a perfectly fine radio in the sitting room."

There was no reply. Faith suspected her mother was look-ing forward to a quiet evening with her only sister.

When the kitchen was clean, Faith and her cousin headed up to the bedroom.

"I want to show you something," said Nell.

She pulled a large black album from under a stack of books on top of the dresser.

"What?" asked Faith.

"It's a family photo album. Thought you'd like to see some of your other relatives from 'round here."

The girls climbed up on the big bouncy bed and began to thumb through the pages, mostly filled with stiff-looking folks in stiff-looking clothes.

"Who's that?" asked Faith, pointing to a tintype picture of an old couple standing ramrod straight in front of the Cole's house.

"That's your Grandma and Grandpa Hackworth. They raised your ma and mine in this house."

"Did you know them?"

"Sure, Grandpa died when I was seven and Granny died in 1922. Your mom came from Seattle for the funeral."

"That's the trip she brought Becky on. She was only two and a half," said Faith.

Nell took her cousin's hand and squeezed hard.

"It was awful, Faith. Your mama having to bury her baby and her mama all on the same day."

Faith didn't know what to say. Her ma and pa never spoke about her dead sister. Faith tried hard to remember her. Becky was nothing but a shadow to her now.

"I can't even remember what she looked like," said Faith. "It makes me so sad. It's almost like she never existed."

FOUR

TUESDAY MORNING WAS CLEAR AND bright. After George left for his morning shift at the railroad switching station down at the Front, Charles, Sadie, Kitty, and the four cousins hiked to a prime huckleberry patch straight up Peach Creek Road. The mountain woods of southern West Virginia had been scrubbed clean. They were all asparkle from the record rains of the day before. Droplets clinging to leaves glittered in the bright sun, and the mountain air felt crisp and fresh.

"This takes me back, hiking these beautiful woods," said Charles. "Girls, look at the trees. You don't see hardwoods like these in the Northwest: beech, oak, dogwood, elm, walnut. We've got our cedars and Doug firs, but they don't top this in my book."

Sadie added, "And the rhodies. Aren't we lucky that they're abloomin' right now?"

Faith breathed in the clean air, earthy from the damp forest floor. Her happiness was palpable. All the stories Papa had told her were now comin' alive.

By noon the buckets were full of the tart berries. After lunch, taking advantage of the still cool day, Nell and Faith started in on a batch of huckleberry jam. Kitty tackled the ironing basket heaped with wrinkled clothes waiting for the sizzle of a hot iron.

"What can I do to help?" asked Sadie.

"Not a thing. Put your feet up," said Kitty.

Sadie took the sewing basket and joined Charles on the front porch. There was always mending to do. She held firm to the belief that idle hands were the devil's workshop.

Marion and Rusty were busy making a bigger home for Broadway out of an old cardboard box. Papa poked holes in the top and sides with an ice pick, and they filled a tuna-fish can with water and lined the floor of the box with grass and leaves.

"Why don't you let the poor thing loose?" asked Faith. "Broadway looks miserable, Marion. He's got no room for hopping."

"I love him, and besides, he'll be able to hop in this box. Look how much bigger it is than the shoe box."

Huckleberry cobbler and jars of jam cooled on the shelf on the screened back porch. The warm, sweet fragrance from the berries wafted through the kitchen. Rusty announced each "pop" as the jam jars sealed.

After supper, Nell talked her father into driving her and Faith into Logan to see the latest picture show, *Cat and the Canary.*

Please let Henry be there, Faith thought.

She couldn't get him out of her head. He was the last thing she thought about at night when she went to bed and the first thing that came to her mind every morning.

He's driving me crazy.

At the ticket line there was a crush of teenagers so absorbed in what they were saying that they didn't look up when the girls got in line.

"What's everyone talking about?" asked Faith.

"I don't know," said Nell. "Hey, Dorothy, what's going on?"

"You mean you haven't heard? It's all over town."

"What's all over town?" asked Nell.

"Billy Butler was up picking berries on Holden Road this morning and found a body in the thicket, a woman named Gloria Gannon. Rumor has it that her throat was slit! Can you believe it? A murder right here in Logan!"

"Who could have done such a thing?" asked Faith to no one in particular. She had never met the murdered woman but she had seen her at the Logan Baptist Church last Sunday morning. Aunt Kitty had pointed her out because she wore a hat that looked like it came from New York City, a smart mauve cloche that sat tilted at an angle on her marcel-waved head.

Just then Faith spotted Henry walking toward them with another boy whom Faith didn't recognize. He was shorter that Henry, sturdy, and solid.

Oh, please, please stop here, thought Faith, as she crossed her fingers behind her back.

"Hey, Henry," shouted Nell. Folks turned to see who the girl was with such a big voice.

Henry nodded at Nell and kept walking toward them. Faith could feel her ears before Henry said a word.

How can I make these darn ears quit this? she thought. *I can't be blushing just at the sight of Henry. He'll think I'm a fool.*

Henry stopped and introduced Walter Fleming to Faith. He was also on the Logan football team, which was easy to tell by his spark-plug build and thick neck.

"Can we cut?" asked Walter.

Faith uncrossed her fingers. Her heart raced in her chest.

Nell said, "Sure. Did you hear about the murder? They found a woman's body up Holden Road."

"Who was it?" asked Walter.

"Dorothy said her name is Gloria Gannon," Nell chimed in. "Her throat . . ."

Faith watched the blood drain from Henry's face. His shoulders slumped.

"You OK, Henry? You look like you've seen a ghost," said Faith. She reached over and, without thinking, put her hand on his, just for a split second.

Henry gulped air, looked at her hand on his, and said, "Yea, it's just that I know her. She and her husband live in our garage apartment. In fact, Gloria was at our house last night for a party. I said hello to her before I went over to Walter's. Are you sure it's her?"

"Not really, right now it's all rumor," said Faith.

"Shouldn't you go home to find out?" asked Nell.

"No, my father would just tell me to stay out of the way and not ask questions. I'll find out soon enough, I guess. I don't know why anyone would want to kill her. She was always nice enough to me. Her husband is a cop and usually has the night shift so she'd come over sometimes in the evening to play cards. She and my mother golf together."

The theater doors opened and the line began to move. Faith turned to see a separate line of Negros waiting behind the white patrons. Henry was right in back of Faith.

Sit next to me, sit next to me, she silently pleaded.

Henry did. Nell made sure she was on Henry's other side. Walter was on the end next to Nell. As soon as the lights went out and the newsreel started with scenes of bread lines and Hooverville in Washington, DC, Henry slid his arm over the back of Faith's seat. He didn't exactly touch her, but all thoughts of a murder on Holden Road vanished. She found it difficult to follow the movie.

Their shoulders touched as they moved closer to each other. Henry lowered his arm at a particularly scary scene in the movie and his hand lightly brushed her shoulder for the last half hour.

I hope he kisses me. No, maybe not. Oh gosh, I wish I knew what I wanted. The kiss didn't happen.

"I hope I see you soon, Faith," said Henry, as Uncle George beeped his horn at them from across the street.

"Me, too."

FIVE

GEORGE DROPPED THE GIRLS BACK home, found his brother-in-law, and the two men lit up their cigars and walked to the Peach Pit. Since prohibition many illegal beer joints had popped up in West Virginia as they had all over the country. The Peach Pit was in the basement of the Peach Creek Boarding House two blocks away. Most of the boarders worked for the C&O Railroad down at the Front, a major switching station for several railroad lines. The men, all regulars at the Pit, had been there since after supper. George worked with many of them.

"Read in the paper that drinking is up since prohibition," said Charles. "Ironic isn't it?"

"It's certainly true around these parts," said George. "Plenty of the railroad men have put a few extra bucks in their pockets by looking the other way when a boxcar full of booze comes through the Front."

Charles and George settled at the bar and ordered their beers.

"Did you hear about the woman who was murdered up Holden Road?" asked George.

"Christ, no. Who was she? When did it happen?"

George replied, "A woman by the name of Gloria Gannon. Her husband's one of the police officers in Logan. Found her body this morning. They live in a garage apartment at the Thompsons' on G Street in Logan. You met Robert Thompson at Peck's Mill that first Sunday you were here."

"Was he that stuffed shirt still dressed in his church clothes who wanted to leave early?"

"Yeah. Works at the Logan First National Bank. I think Gloria worked there, too. Heard he got her the job. She was quite a looker and she knew it. Strutted those long legs of hers all over town. I think every man in Logan wanted to get in her pants."

"But why would anyone want to kill her?"

"Oh, come on, Charles. There were plenty of men who might want her dead. I don't want Kitty or Sadie to hear this, but there's a key club in Logan above the five-and-dime."

"No kidding," said Charles.

"Lots of bigwigs belong. Make a list of the church elders, the city council, and all the bankers, lawyers, and doctors, then throw in most of the mine owners and foremen in the county, and you've got the membership."

Charles took a swig of cold beer and said, "You think her murder is connected to the key club?"

"Hard to say."

Charles smoothed out the *Tribune* lying on the counter and pointed to the headline on the sports page. It read "I Was Robbed!"

"They're right. Sharkey beat Schmeling to a pulp. He shoulda won."

George nodded in agreement. "No question it was a fix. About the murder—I bet someone from the key club is somehow mixed up in this murder. Lots of shenanigans going on up there and word is Gloria was seen there more than once. Heard she was slit from ear to ear. Probably dumped up on Holden Road last night. That's my guess." George grabbed a handful of peanuts and continued.

"Let's don't talk about this in front of the family," said Charles. "Gossip's already flying. Nell said that's all anyone was talking about at the picture show tonight. The less the women and children hear, the better."

"It's going to be rough when all the dirt comes out. This is going to be a scandal to beat all scandals, you just watch," said George.

They finished their beers and walked home in the dark.

Late the following afternoon Charles drove to Logan to buy a paper. The *Logan Tribune* headlines screamed "Woman's Body Found Off Holden Road Near Trace Mountain." The account filled in details and answered rumors. The paper read:

> Gloria Gannon's body was found about ten yards down an embankment on Trace Mountain. It most likely wouldn't have been noticed if the huckleberries hadn't ripened early. The authorities believe she died sometime Monday night, and the body was dumped there during the early morning. A young boy, Billy Butler, found the body while out picking berries about nine thirty on Tuesday morning.

Gloria was described as wearing a blue-and-white polka-dot dress with a turban style hat to match. She was missing her shoes but her pocketbook was found beside her. It contained twenty dollars, a pack of cigarettes, a tube of lipstick, and a silver compact. There was an expensive gold watch around her left wrist. Everything was covered in mud. Officers did not believe robbery was a motive. Rape was not ruled out but would have to wait for the autopsy for confirmation. Most disturbing was the fact that her neck appeared to be broken and her throat had been slit from ear to ear.

Charles swung by the Front on the way home and picked up George.

"What's the latest?" asked George, as he slid into the seat of the pickup and picked up the paper to read the headlines.

"They've arrested Thompson and his handyman, Williams," said Charles. "Sheriff found blood in the back of the car that Sidney hauled the dogs in, and they got bloody rags from the Thompson basement. Doesn't look good for either of 'em."

George drew in his breath with a low whistle as he read the front page on the way home. When he got home George threw the paper on the couch without thinking. Charles later found Faith totally engrossed in the front page.

"Papa, I can't believe it. Henry's dad has been arrested and so has Sidney. To think that Marion was rescued by a man accused of murder, and Mama and Aunt Kitty were at League just the week before at the Thompsons'," said Faith. "Why would Mr. Thompson want to kill that lady?"

"Sweet Pea, it's all just speculation. Nothing has been proved yet."

"And what about the colored fellow. He was really nice. He was so shy and he was very mannerly to us both. He wouldn't even take a glass of iced tea. We had to insist that he take the leftover pound cake. He just couldn't have done such a thing, I'm sure of it."

"Faith, it's best you just put the whole matter out of your mind. This is adult business and none of it concerns you," Papa said.

Faith puffed up and replied, "Quit treating me like a baby! I'm almost eighteen." Charles watched as she stormed up the stairs to Nell's room, slamming the door behind her.

SIX

"THERE'S BEEN SOME TROUBLE UP at Holden 2 Mine," said Uncle George as Faith sat down at the table. "I got a call from my brother, Ralph. He's coming from Charleston to see if he can work something out between the union and the owners. It's been a few days since the mine collapsed. The owners are already throwing the mine widows out of their homes and their husbands still warm in their graves. Looks like Ralph could be here a while."

"Thank the Lord you don't work in the mines. Will Ralph be staying with his sister Elizabeth?" asked Kitty. "We should have them over for dinner on Sunday."

'Who're Ralph and Elizabeth?" asked Marion.

"She's the one who's having the party for Mama's birthday," said Nell. "Remember?"

Marion was sitting at the dining room table after supper coloring with her brand-new box of crayons that Mama had bought her on a whim at the five-and-dime. Rusty was snugged up in a chair listening to *The Lone Ranger* on the radio.

Uncle George explained, "Elizabeth and Ralph are my sister and brother. They aren't really related to you, Marion, but you can call Elizabeth 'Aunt Liz' just like Nell and Rusty. She'd like that," said George. "Elizabeth lives in Logan."

"She lives in a mansion," piped in Nell.

"Nell, it's not polite to talk about people's money," said Kitty.

"Well, it's true. Wait till you see the house, Faith. They've got stained-glass windows and crystal lights shipped over from Italy, and indoor plumbing, and Persian carpets."

"Shhh, I can't hear the radio," said Rusty, turning up the volume. Everyone ignored him.

"Ralph is bringing his daughter Cecelia with him," George continued, ignoring Rusty. "Cecelia's mom just left to spend a month in Arizona. The dry desert air should be good for her lungs. Elizabeth is hoping Cecelia will stay for the rest of the summer. I think it's lonely for Elizabeth and Morris rattling around in that big old house, just the two of them and the colored help."

"It's a shame they never had children. Lord knows they tried. Losing all those babies before they were born. So much heartache," said Sadie.

"Ralph still work for the United Mine Workers?" asked Charles.

"Yes," said Kitty. "Now he's their head lawyer. The mine owners hate him almost as much as John Lewis, the union organizer. Ralph's had some death threats, and with that and the Lindberg kidnapping this spring, he's hired guards to protect Cecelia. They drive her to school in a limousine. Seems a bit over the top, if you ask me, but they can afford it, I guess."

Faith was taking everything in while she worked on a pale green shawl she was crocheting for her Aunt Kitty. Kitty didn't know it was to be a birthday gift. The edge was intricate, and Faith was forever pulling out the trim when she missed a stitch.

"How old is Cecelia?" she asked.

Nell was quick to respond. "Sixteen, a year younger than us, and she's spoiled rotten. She gets anything she wants. They live on a big farm, just outside Charleston. She has her own horse and even a donkey from Mexico."

George let out a big belly laugh at the mention of the donkey. "Now there's a story if I ever heard one."

"Tell us, pa. Tell us the story," said Rusty.

Sadie looked at George and said, "Yes, tell us the story."

George continued, "All right, but, Rusty, you've heard this story more than once." He winked at the young man. "Seems Ralph was sitting in some back room with a couple of cronies when one of them up and says he's traveling down to Mexico. 'What kind of souvenir you want me to send you?' the lawyer friend asked Ralph. Without missing a beat, Ralph told the fellow to send him a goddamn jackass.

"And sure enough, a month later here comes a telegram to be at the Charleston train station to pick up a package. Ralph goes down to the station on the appointed day, and there waitin' for him is a big wooden crate with a little Mexican burro's head hanging out one end and his ass out the other. I'll be damned if that lawyer didn't send Ralph his jackass!"

The whole table erupted in laughter. It rolled out with snorts and tears, and it took a while for everyone to regain their composure. "George, shame on you. You need to watch your language, there are children at the table," chided Aunt Kitty, holding back laughter.

Sadie, drying her eyes on her apron, said, "Well, I'm looking forward to seeing Ralph. It's been quite a while. And as for you, Nell, Cecelia is your cousin. I wouldn't be so hard on her. She can't be held responsible for an accident of birth, you know."

In their room, Nell couldn't wait to cover more territory about her cousin Cecelia.

"They've got three colored women working for them: a cook, a housekeeper, and a woman to do the wash. And that's not all. There's a foreman to run the barn, and a couple of men work under him. I honestly don't know what Cecelia's mom does all day. Mama says her health isn't good. Cecelia was raised for her first four years by a colored nanny whose name was Minny. The only mother Cecelia knew was Minny. She even called her 'Mama.' Can you imagine going to school in a limousine every day? How dreamy is that?"

"Even as crabby as Mama is sometimes, I wouldn't have wanted her to be gone for four years, I don't care how much money I had. When do you think we'll get to see your Aunt Elizabeth's house? I've never been in a mansion."

"If Cecelia really does spend the rest of the summer in Logan, we'll be invited over a lot. Aunt Liz is really fun. She loves to throw parties. Last year she had a Valentine's Day party and I got to help her deck the whole house out in red. She served a red fruit punch and red velvet cupcakes with red icing and Red Hots on top. I cut hearts out of paper doilies and red foil and plastered them on all the windows. Everyone in town was invited."

"Wow, I wish I could have seen it. So, do you think I'll like Cecelia?"

"Maybe. She's so quiet, she's always got her nose stuck in a book, and she thinks she's better than everyone else. You'll get your chance to check her out on Sunday 'cause it sounds like Mama is inviting them all for Sunday dinner," said Nell.

SEVEN

AFTER SUPPER, GEORGE AND CHARLES settled in to the parlor chairs as Sadie and Kitty cleaned up the supper dishes and settled the children in bed before joining their husbands. The room was already filled with tobacco smoke, and peach brandy sat on a side table ready to be opened. After pouring a glass for everyone except Sadie, who was a strict Baptist and never drank, Kitty quickly turned the conversation to Gloria Gannon's murder.

The latest rumor to surface was that Gloria and Mr. Thompson were having an affair. "I heard that a straight razor was found in the Thompsons' basement," said Kitty, as she took a little sip of her peach brandy. "The *Tribune* said that not only was Gloria's throat slit, but her neck was broken as well."

"Wouldn't put too much stock in the razor. Someone told me Sidney slept in the attic but cleaned up in the basement laundry tub. But no question someone really must have wanted her dead," said George. "Everything leads to Robert Thompson, if you ask me: blood in the basement and blood in the Ford. Some of the fellows at work said that someone hosed the car down. Thompson's got a hell of a motive, too. I bet Mrs. Thompson found out her husband was stepping out on her with that Gannon woman right under her nose."

Charles thought, *So much for not talking to the womenfolk about the scandal.*

And then he plunged on in himself.

"I'm not so sure. Why would he kill two ways? And what about Sidney, the colored handyman? I just don't think a Negro would kill a white woman. That's a lynching for sure, guaranteed."

Sadie put down her coffee and looked at Charles. "Explain to me just what goes on at a key club and don't leave anything out. I'm having trouble understanding all of this, how Christian men and women could do such horrible things."

"You know too much already," said Charles. "Everyone isn't as gosh-fearing as you are. There's an awful lot of sinning going on, and it's usually the least expected that are doing the sinning."

"For goodness sake, Charles. I've birthed three children. I think I can handle a little sinning."

The room went quiet, and the air was heavy. It was rare that Kitty and George heard mention of Sadie's lost child, even if it was unintentional. Sadie herself looked stunned as she picked up her sewing and headed to the bedroom. Charles followed her, leaving his peach brandy behind.

"Wait, Sadie," he called after her.

She didn't turn around but continued down the hall. When she got to their room she slammed the door. Thank goodness Marion was a hard sleeper. She only stirred and rolled over in her cot under the window at the other end of the room.

"Sadie, what's got you so riled up? I've never seen you like this. Is it the murder?"

Sadie's hands were balled up in tight fists. Her cheeks were flushed as she met Charles's eyes. "That and other things. I don't like being treated like a child. Don't ever talk to me like that again."

Charles knew better than to push her to tell him what else was bothering her, but he knew it was wrapped up with baby Becky. In the eleven years since the awful events of the train ride to Peach Creek and back, Charles and Sadie had never talked about it. There had been an exchange of horrible telegrams regarding Becky's death and burial arrangements, but that was it. Sadie came home a changed woman. The light was out of her eyes, and she turned to the Bible for comfort, which never came. The longer the silence, the harder it was to broach the subject. Becky's death became a wall that grew brick by brick, higher and higher with each passing month and each passing year. Even when Sadie got pregnant with Marion two years after Becky's death, the wall remained. Charles had been hopeful this new child would soften the grief, but it didn't. Sadie retreated even further. Marion was the light of his world and Faith's too, but Sadie didn't seem to see her.

Marion kept everyone laughing with her antics and physical feats. She was walking at nine months, climbing up on anything in sight when she was just a year, and once she had a few words she could string together, there wasn't a moment of silence around the house. The family was living in the logging camp where Charles worked cutting down the old growth Douglas firs that grew thick, tall, and majestic throughout Puget Sound. Marion spent most days out in the clearings. She loved the birds, squirrels, and other forest creatures that shared their home with the loggers. Marion feared nothing, befriending every animal that lived in the woods.

Sadie left the real mothering to Faith and Charles, which they took on willingly. Sadie contented herself with wifely chores: cooking, washing, sewing, and her Bible. In the eleven years since Becky's death, nothing had lifted the black cloud hovering over Sadie's head.

The couple changed into their nightclothes without a word between them and lay down on the double bed. Sadie rolled away from Charles and pulled the light summer quilt tightly up under her neck. It was clear to Charles that Sadie wasn't going to talk tonight and that he was going to have to do a whole lot of sweet-talking to get back in her good graces. In order to thaw Sadie's icy response, Charles was going to have to start telling her the whole truth about those key clubs and all the other underworld business that was going on in Logan County. Charles listened to the riot of bullfrogs down by the creek. He knew that neither he nor Sadie would fall asleep any time soon, and it wasn't the bullfrogs keeping them awake.

EIGHT

THE TABLE WAS SET FOR Sunday dinner with the good china with roses and a gold rim that had belonged to Granny Hackworth. An exuberant bouquet of summer roses filled a tall cut-glass vase in the center of the table. Berry pies were cooling on the kitchen windowsill, and dirty dishes sat scraped and rinsed in the sink.

"Who's ready for dessert?" asked Kitty.

"Did you make that famous berry pie, Kitty?" said her brother-in-law, Ralph.

Ralph and his daughter, Cecelia, had driven over to Peach Creek with George's sister Elizabeth and her husband Morris right after church on Sunday.

"Isn't it grand to have so many of our kin at one table?" exclaimed George. He was clearly proud to be hosting Sunday dinner.

"I didn't know we had so many relatives," said Marion.

"Well, technically we're more like kissin' cousins to George's family," said Charles. "But I'm happy to claim them as our own."

After the kitchen was cleaned up and dinner dishes put away, Kitty, Sadie, and Elizabeth gathered on the porch while the men and Marion and Rusty went out back to pitch horseshoes. Nell, Faith, and Cecelia sat on the porch steps with the womenfolk. The talk turned to the murder.

"Morris and I were at the Thompsons' Monday night, the night they claim Gloria Gannon was murdered," said Elizabeth.

The women gasped in unison. "What were you doing over there?" asked Kitty.

"The Thompsons were having a get-together and invited us. It was mostly Robert's banking friends, although Dr. Colridge and his wife were there along with the new dentist in town. The men were listening to the big fight and drinking whiskey and the womenfolk were sipping cocktails in the dining room by the fireplace. It's really lovely with a thick granite mantel. Gloria was there, but her husband was on duty, I think," said Elizabeth. "We left early because there was just too much drinking for me."

"Wouldn't it be swell to have a fireplace in the dining room? Our winters are so cold. What was Gloria wearing?" Kitty asked.

"Let me think. Oh, it was quite modern, a short blue polka-dot dress—I think it was silk with a matching hat."

Nell responded, "That's what she was wearing when they found her body!"

When the conversation shifted to more mundane topics, the girls decided to take a walk up Peach Creek Road. The heat of the day hung into the late afternoon, and the girls hoped it might be cooler under the big trees in the woods. Not a leaf moved on the old oaks, dogwoods, and alders, sprinkled with the occasional scrub pine. By the time the teenage girls had reached the deepest woods, Faith was soaked to her underwear, sweat dripping between her breasts and down her back.

"If it's this hot in June, I can't imagine what it will be like by August," she said. "How do you stand it? Even on the hottest days in August, there's always a cool breeze blowing off Puget Sound."

"I guess we just get used to it. We don't know any different," said Cecelia.

Faith had listened to Nell bait Cecelia all through dinner and as they were cleaning up after dinner.

"It must be nice to have a maid do all the cooking and cleaning," Nell had said as she wiped one of the china plates with a flour-sack towel.

Either Cecelia didn't know what Nell was doing, or this rich cousin of Nell's from Charleston chose to ignore her. Faith was uncomfortable hearing Nell, but it was easy to see why Nell might be jealous. Cecelia was as beautiful as Nell. Her long blond hair hung in perfect, soft waves around her face. Faith couldn't find a pimple on her face, just a perfect peaches-and-cream complexion. Her eyes were large and the purest, almost unreal, emerald green. She was tall like her father with long legs just like her cousin. Her only physical fault, as far as Faith could tell, was that she was flat chested, but when Faith thought of her own body, a small bust seemed like an asset.

Nell continued to press Cecelia. "Tell Faith about all your horses and how you perform at all the football games."

"Oh, she wouldn't be interested in that. I'd much rather hear about what it's like to live out West."

Faith said, "You tell me about the football games, and I promise I'll bore you with my life in Seattle."

"All right," said Cecelia. "Well, I have this little Mexican burro named Petey-O-Phidelius. I've had him since I was seven. At halftime at football games, there is always a parade and I ride Petey-O around the outside track of the football field in front of the band and the cheerleaders. I wear a big sombrero with pom-poms bouncing around the brim."

Cecelia laughed. "I guess I'm quite a sight. My legs have gotten so long I have to hold them up off the ground the whole way. I look pretty much like a fool, but Petey-O and I have become somewhat of a tradition. Not sure what will happen when I graduate next year. Maybe we'll have to loan him out for the home games in the fall until he gets too old to parade at halftime."

Faith loved that Cecelia laughed at herself thinking about the spectacle she and Petey-O made on the field.

Nell was hardly listening, appearing to be more interested in something across the other side of Peach Creek. This part of the little creek was running slowly with only a few feet of water, but it did look inviting on such a sweltering afternoon.

"I think I see some blackberries on the other side. I'm going across to pick some. I'll be right back."

Faith watched as Nell took off her shoes and stockings, hitched up her skirt, and ventured out into the cool water. It was only up to her knees, even in the middle. Faith was still smiling at the thought of Cecelia on that donkey parading around the football field. She wiped the sweat on her face with the hem of her skirt. By the time Nell climbed the bank on the other side of the creek, Faith and Cecelia were on to the topic of life in Seattle. Despite the fact that Faith considered her own life quite mundane, Cecelia seemed fascinated. Faith told stories of Broadway Lunch and her Papa's parrot.

"Papa trained the parrot to yell, 'Hey, Charles. Bring me a goddamn beer,' on cue when the cable car lets passengers off in front of the store," said Faith.

Cecelia laughed at the tale in a peculiar high-pitched squeal. Faith continued to watch as Nell walked gingerly to where the tiny black caps were rambling over a dead tree stump. The rare little jewels of fruit were perfectly ripe. Nell had found them ahead of the birds. Then Nell scrambled over a log and Faith lost sight of her.

Nell is being so rude, thought Faith, but she didn't want to say anything to Cecelia.

She continued her tale of learning to swim in Puget Sound and how the salt water made her more buoyant.

"Is that really possible?' said Cecelia.

"Of course it is," said Faith, "although if you're built like I am you have an added advantage." Faith stuck out her ample chest as both girls got the giggles.

"Where's Nell? Do you see her?" asked Cecelia, gasping for breath.

"She can't be far. Don't tell her I said this, but I think she was miffed because you were getting all the attention. Nell believes the moon and the stars orbit around her," said Faith.

"Let's go find her," said Cecelia. "I don't want to hurt her feelings."

How can Nell not like Cecelia? She's not got a mean bone in her body, thought Faith.

The two girls pulled off their shoes and stockings, tucked their skirts in their waistbands, and waded across the creek carrying their shoes. The water felt refreshingly cool.

"Nell? Nell, where are you?" asked Faith, cupping her hands and calling Nell's name again.

The two girls heard Nell's weak voice, "Over here."

Faith and Cecelia looked up the hill and spotted Nell lying close to a large rock. They immediately scrambled up to where Nell had fallen. Cecelia bent down, looked at Nell's swollen ankle, and immediately knew what had happened.

Cecelia barked orders. "Lie still, Nell. You're going to be all right. Faith, run home and tell Daddy and Uncle George and your Pa to get up here quick, and bring a blanket. I think she's going into shock."

"What's wrong? Did she break something?"

"No, snakebite."

"Oh, my gosh!"

Faith took off running down the hill barefoot, heart racing. She remembered her Papa's snake story.

Faith found the men still out back throwing horseshoes.

"Hurry, Nell's been bit by a snake!"

Faith was shaking with fear.

George called to Kitty, "Call Doc Howard and have him get here fast!"

Charles ran inside and pulled a blanket off George and Kitty's bed, then rushed back outside.

In a matter of minutes, the men were up the hill and at Nell's side. Faith followed, panting in the heat, her feet bleeding. The three men lifted Nell up and placed the blanket underneath her. George took a pocketknife out of his back pocket and flipped it open. He held a match to the blade, then drew the knife across his daughter's ankle where the snake had broken the skin. Faith watched, frozen, as Nell flinched. As soon as he saw blood, George leaned over and began to suck out the blood. He spit it out and sucked again and spit again.

He spent a good five minutes doing this until Charles put his hand on his brother-in-law's shoulder and said, "OK, George. I think we'd better get her down the hill. She's lookin' mighty pale. Wrap her up, and Ralph and I will carry her. We need to keep her flat. You girls go ahead and tell Kitty to get a poultice ready."

Cecelia had both Nell's and Faith's shoes and stockings in her hand. Faith pulled her shoes on without bothering to put her stockings on, too. She tried to tie the laces, but her feet were swollen, and she could feel how tender and scraped up the soles of her feet were. Cecelia quickly pulled on her own shoes and waded across the stream. Faith watched as the fine cream-colored leather stained a dark brown as the lovely shoes got wet.

"You better go ahead, Cecelia. I can't move very fast on these feet."

No one thought to ask about the snake: where was it, was it still alive, what kind was it?

The men carried Nell over the trail as quickly as they possibly could, knowing how important it was to keep her heart higher than her feet. The deadly poison would kill her for sure if it got to her heart, although that was fairly rare in these parts. The biggest danger was losing a toe or a foot, or, worse yet, a leg.

"Papa, look at her foot. It's so swollen up," said Faith.

Nell was moaning. "Papa, it hurts. Help me, I can't bear it." Her whole body began to shake and she broke out into a cold sweat—not the shivers Faith had seen when she got back to her. Now she was writhing.

"Shhh, baby. You're going to be fine. Just lie still and we'll be home in no time," said George.

George was nearly as pale as his daughter. As soon as the men got Nell home, they placed her on the sofa in the sitting room. It had only taken twenty minutes from the time Faith told them the news until they had Nell home, but in that short time her symptoms worsened. She began to throw up. When Kitty unwrapped the blanket to clean the wound, she gasped.

"Oh, God help us," she whispered.

Nell's foot had swollen to more than twice its size, and the skin had an unnatural shine to it. Worse still, it was already black-and-blue and bruised.

Faith held Nell's hand. It was clammy. Nell's teeth were chattering and she shook uncontrollably.

"Mama, help me. It hurts so bad. Am I going to die?"

"No, no. You'll be fine. Doc Howard will be here soon. Lie still, honey, just lie still. We're going to put a poultice on your ankle. It will be OK."

Sadie was all business. She put a clean towel under Nell's leg, Charles pulled a cloth out of the coffee can that he and George used for a spittoon when they chewed tobacco on the porch. He folded the vile, soaked cloth in half and in half again and placed it gently over the bite. Then Sadie wrapped the towel over the poultice. "I know this works, Kitty."

"Where is he?" whispered George.

Sadie motioned for him to follow her to the kitchen. Faith overheard their conversation even though her mother spoke in a hushed voice. "I called as soon as Faith told me the news. Mrs. Howard answered the phone. She said Doc Howard was up at Little Creek, fishing with their son. She was going to send a neighbor up to fetch him, but I think it will take a while. Lord, I hope he gets here in time."

"Don't even think that, Sadie. Nell's going to be fine."

"I'm sure we are doing all we can. We'll keep the poultice on the bite, and let it do its job," said Charles.

Faith could see the fear written all over Kitty's face.

"Kitty, remember when I got bit as a boy, and our pa stuck my foot in a bucket of tobacco juice, and it pulled all the poison right out," said Charles.

Kitty nodded and placed a cool cloth on Nell's forehead. Nell moaned and threw up again.

"Go to the kitchen and get some wet cloths and a basin, Faith," said Sadie. "And check on Marion and Rusty. Cecelia is on the porch with them. I don't want them in here at all. They shouldn't see this. Get them all some lemonade and sugar cookies and take out the crayons and some paper to keep them busy. And then come straight back in here. I'll need you."

Faith looked down at Nell. Kitty was by her side trying to keep her calm. Nell's face was contorted with pain. Her ankle was darker and more swollen if that was even possible.

"I think we'd better try a tourniquet above the bite. It should help slow the flow of the poison. Just don't tie it too tight," said Charles. "Kitty, have you got an old sheet we can use?"

"Look in the linen closet upstairs next to Nell's room. The old sheets are on the bottom shelf with the towels I use for rags."

Ralph ran upstairs and came down with the sheets. Faith went to the kitchen to get cookies and lemonade for Rusty and Marion. She gathered up the crayons and some butcher paper and went out to the back porch.

"What's going on?" said Rusty. "I want to see my sister."

"Not right now. Aunt Kitty said to stay out here with Marion for the time being. Nell's going to be OK. The doctor is on his way," said Faith. "Cecelia, are you all right out here with the kids?"

"Sure, whatever Aunt Kitty wants me to do."

Faith quickly returned to the parlor to find her mother tearing a sheet up into long strips. Charles took one and wrapped it above Nell's calf, tying it in a knot. Nell whimpered. She was too weak to scream.

What if she dies? thought Faith. *Stop, just stop it, you idiot.*

Charles went to find another blanket even though it was a hot summer afternoon. As he headed up the stairs, Faith looked out the front window to see a middle-aged man carrying a black leather bag heading for the door.

"Dr. Howard's here, I think," she said.

The doctor was still dressed in his fishing cloths—old overalls and knee-high rubber boots. He put his wide-brimmed straw hat on the table by the door and walked in.

"Let's have a look at her. Everyone please step back."

By now Charles was back down with the second blanket, but he just stood there with it in his arms like a dead cat, as Dr. Howard lifted the blanket, unwrapped the towel, and took off the tobacco spit poultice. Tenderly, he felt around the wound.

"How long since the bite? When did the poultice go on?"

Kitty filled him in on the details, never taking her hand off Nell's forehead.

"Ma'am," said the doctor, looking at Sadie but not remembering her name, "Please go and put a teaspoon of baking soda and a teaspoon of salt in a quart of cool water. Mix it well and bring it in here. We need to get some fluids in the girl. She's gone into shock. And put the kettle on to boil. I need to clean the wound now."

There was a scurry of activity as Dr. Howard proceeded to clean the bitten area with alcohol and cotton. It seemed to go on forever. In reality, the doctor had the area cleaned in just a few minutes. Sadie came back with the cool water mixture and a pan of boiling water. Dr. Howard showed Kitty how to soak clean rags in the hot water, then wrap them over the wound to pull the infection from the leg.

"Keep the clean rags on until they cool, then put a small amount of ointment on the wound, cover it with another strip of clean sheet, and wrap the wound. You'll have to do this four times a day until the swelling goes down and the bite begins to heal over," said the doctor.

Next he took a teaspoon of the soda/salt water and put the spoon to Nell's lips. She was too weak and delirious to drink, so the doctor opened her lips and poured it in. Nell gagged and sputtered, and most of it spilled.

"Don't worry, if you can't get much down. Just try a little bit every half hour. Any liquid is better than none. We can't let her get dehydrated or her kidneys will begin to fail. Just keep trying. I'm afraid that you will all have to take turns through the night. We can't leave her alone for a minute. It shouldn't be hard with all of you living here."

With that he got up and turned to George.

"Did anyone see the snake? It would be good if we were sure what kind it was."

Dr. Howard looked down at Nell, who, although she was still breathing shallowly, appeared to be resting more comfortably.

George said, "Let me get Cecelia. She and Faith got to Nell soon after it happened."

Cecelia came in from the porch followed right behind by Marion and Rusty. Their eyes zeroed in on Nell. They stared at her with their mouths open.

"Don't be too alarmed, children. Nell's not out of the woods, but Dr. Howard has given her excellent care. And we're all here to take care of her. Right now she just needs to rest. The doctor gave her something to help her sleep and to get her through the pain," said Sadie.

Marion and Rusty stood side by side as if their bones were locked in place.

"Girls," began Dr. Howard, looking at Faith and Cecelia. "Did either of you see the snake that bit Nell? It would be helpful if we could identify it, so we are sure we are treating the bite correctly."

Faith shivered and shook her head no. Cecelia spoke up. "I'm positive it was a copperhead."

"How can you be so sure?" asked the doctor.

"Cecelia knows her poisonous snakes," Ralph piped up. "She needed to know what to do in case she or her horse got bit. She knows her stuff."

All eyes were now on Cecelia. She looked up and proceeded to tell her story.

"After Faith ran down to get you all, I heard a rustling behind the big rock where Nell fell. I saw the biggest copperhead I'd ever seen, and he looked mad. His head was raised, and he was looking straight at me with those cat eyes they have. As quick as I could, I picked up the first rock I saw and threw it as hard as I could at his head."

There was a collective intake of air as she continued.

"I think I stunned him, but I could tell he wasn't dead so I found another rock and hit him again. The second rock was bigger, and I think it pretty much crushed his skull."

Cecelia was looking at Nell on the couch.

Faith looked at Cecelia in awe.

"You're so brave. I honestly don't know what I would have done in your shoes, but I sure as heck couldn't have killed him," said Faith.

"You are, indeed, a very brave girl," said Aunt Kitty. "We are so grateful you were there, Cecelia. You saved our Nell."

She put her arms around Cecelia's slender body and hugged her tight. All the tears that Kitty had been holding in came, at that moment, in a flood.

Cecelia patted her aunt's back. "It's OK, Aunt Kitty, it's OK. Nell will come through this. I just know she will."

Sadie said, "I think we should all say a prayer for Nell."

The group gathered around Nell lying on the sofa and joined hands. They bowed their heads, and Sadie prayed, "Dear Jesus, we thank you for saving Nell's life from that viper, and we thank you for sending us Cecelia. Please bless her for her strength and courage. Please don't let Nell die, we pray."

A chorus of amens filled the parlor.

NINE

FAITH WAS STANDING ON THE porch alone in the dark. She was still wearing a pink gingham apron tied around her waist even though the supper dishes were washed and put away. Her unruly red curls weren't quite all caught up in a ribboned ponytail. Her eyes were swollen. She wiped them with the back of her hand.

"Hey, Faith, is that you?" Henry said, as he waved slightly.

"Henry, what are you doing out here on a Wednesday night?" Faith straightened her skirt and untied the apron. "Come on up."

There was no sign of anyone else in the big blue house. All the lights were off except for one in Nell's window upstairs.

"Where is everyone?" asked Henry.

"Everyone's pretty exhausted. We're all taking shifts. Mother is up with Nell right now, and I'm spelling her in an hour. Papa and Uncle George are down at the Peach Pit. It's the first night they've been out in a week. The little kids and Aunt Kitty are sleeping."

"Whoa! Wait a minute. What's wrong with Nell?" asked Henry.

Henry looked at Faith, and she knew he could see her swollen bloodshot eyes.

Faith said, "She was bitten by a copperhead last Sunday about a half mile up Peach Creek. It's been touch and go ever since. She went into shock, her foot is still swollen terribly, and she's in unbearable pain."

Henry grabbed her hand and squeezed it hard.

"I had no idea. Why didn't someone tell me?"

He stopped and dropped her hand.

"We've been so busy tending to Nell day and night since Sunday when it happened that we haven't been to Logan or anywhere but right here.

"Can I see her?"

Faith shook her head.

"Doc Howard said no visitors. He gave her some medicine for the pain and something else to help her sleep. She's out of it most of the time, and when she's awake she doesn't seem to know what's going on. Mother says the best thing for her right now is rest."

Faith gulped and slid over on the porch swing. Henry sat next to her, as close as when they were at the movies. He put his arm across her shoulders. Then, without warning he tenderly pushed the stray curls out of Faith's eyes and tucked them behind her ears. She began to cry, not big crocodile tears, just soft little sobs. Faith leaned into Henry, and he wrapped his arm a little tighter. They sat like this for some time. The bullfrogs were singing up a storm and the occasional firefly lit up the night sky. It was a perfect summer evening. The porch swing squeaked quietly as Henry stroked her hair and patted her shoulder.

"Shhh, it's OK. She'll be OK."

"I don't know, Henry. It was awful. Cecelia and I were with her. Cecelia killed it with a rock. She smashed its head. I've never seen a snake that big. We don't have poisonous snakes back home. Cecelia's dad went up there and brought the thing back. It was huge. Poor Marion has had nightmares every night since."

Faith sat up and looked at Henry. She had totally forgotten about his father and the murder.

"I'm sorry. How are you? Do you want to talk about what's going on?"

"I'm not sure. I finally got my father to tell me some stuff tonight. Up until then, no one would tell me anything." said Henry. "Mother doesn't come down from her room. It's like she's paralyzed. My little sisters are being shipped off to my grandparents in Huntington tomorrow for the rest of the summer, because mother can't seem to cope with anything. I haven't seen any of my buddies in days. The worst part is that strangers stand in front of our house and just stare, waiting for someone to come out. Some of them even take pictures of the house. It's awful."

Faith didn't say anything. They just sat quietly, listening to the night sounds around them.

"I'd better go. I'll come check on you and Nell tomorrow."

Henry stood up, as did Faith. He bent down, she stood on her tiptoes, and they kissed gently on the lips. It seemed as natural as breathing.

TEN

GRADUALLY, NELL SHOWED SIGNS OF improvement. She was drinking on her own, the swelling on her ankle wasn't as pronounced, and she didn't require round-the-clock care. Still, the mood at the Cole house was subdued and sad. Up until now, Nell had not been able to give an account of what had happened up in the woods on that Sunday afternoon. On Saturday afternoon, a week after the accident, everyone in the family was gathered around Nell's bed. Sadie thought it was important to pray over Nell each day.

Even Charles took part. "I figure it can't hurt," he said.

"I think I'm ready to tell the story now," said Nell, as Sadie said her final amen. "I thought I could pick enough black caps to make a tart. I knew you'd be pleased, Mama. So I held my skirt in my left hand as a makeshift bucket. When I cleaned out that first patch, I proceeded farther up the hill, and when my skirt was full, I turned to go back down."

Nell took a sip of water and was ready to continue her story.

"Don't tire yourself, Nell," said Kitty. "You can finish later. Maybe you should rest."

I know why you really crossed the creek to pick berries, Faith thought. *You couldn't stand that Cecelia had the spotlight.*

"I'd like to finish," said Nell. "I was almost back to that first rock when I felt the pain. It was as if a knife had been shoved into my ankle, a knife whose tip was afire. It happened so fast and it didn't let up. It got worse when I tried to put weight on the ankle. I stumbled and fell to the ground. That's when I saw him." Nell took a deep breath and paused for dramatic effect. "A copperhead at least three feet long was coiled up next to the rock. The snake's head was up, his tongue was flicking in and out, and he was staring at me."

Marion put her hands over her ears. "Oh, I can't hear any more. It's too scary," she said.

"I don't know what you're so scared about," said Rusty. "We all know how it turns out!"

The tension was broken as everyone laughed nervously. Nell was visibly disappointed that the dramatic effect had disappeared, but she continued on. "The viper must have been sunning himself on the rock, and I guess I disturbed him picking berries right under his nose. I was afraid to move or make a sound for fear the copperhead would strike again. He was shaking his tail, and I heard a soft but distinct rattling noise. I knew I had to stay calm so the venom wouldn't travel to my heart and kill me." She paused for dramatic effect. "That's when I heard Faith call my name, thank the Lord."

Marion's eyes were huge, and she was frozen to the floor.

Charles looked at Marion's face and said to her, "I'm going to the lumberyard to pick up some fencing for the back. Why don't you come with your pa? I think a change of scene would do you a heap of good. Rusty, you come, too."

"Good idea. Let's all leave and let Nell rest a bit," said Kitty. "I think we could all use a change of scenery. That was quite a tale, Sweetheart. I'm just happy I didn't hear the whole thing until we knew that you were on the mend. You'll be tellin' that story to your grandbabies." Kitty placed a cool cloth on Nell's forehead, and everyone left the room.

When Charles and the two younger cousins got back to Peach Creek, fence posts tied in the truck bed, Charles had made a decision. "Sadie, pack up the girls. We're going to Ironton tomorrow to see my sister. Been thinking this is a good time for a visit. Maybe we can even get up in the hills and see Great Uncle John. I'd like the girls to meet him."

"I've been thinking the same thing. Nell's out of the woods and I think Kitty might like to have the house to herself for a bit. And Faith and Marion need a break" said Sadie. "They deserve a little fun after caring for Nell and doing extra chores, and, poor Marion, she's having nightmares."

The next morning Charles lifted the grip Sadie had packed for the week.

"What's in here, rocks?"

Sadie laughed. "A few jars of huckleberry jam, and a packet of your smoked salmon from home, oh, and the pillow slips I embroidered for Alma."

Marion left Broadway in Rusty's care with strict instructions to give him fresh bugs every day and, no matter what, not to let him out of his box. They all kissed Kitty good-bye.

"We'll be home in a week. Sure you'll be OK?" asked Sadie. Charles assured Kitty he would get that fence rebuilt as soon as they got back.

Then he watched Faith as she stood by Nell at the side of the sofa where she was spending most days now.

"I feel guilty leaving you here. I wish you could come with us. Maybe I should stay," said Faith.

"Don't be a jackass. Of course you are going. You haven't met any of your father's family. I'll be fine. Mother said Uncle Ralph is bringing Cecelia out for a visit this week. It will give me a chance to properly thank her. Maybe she's not so bad after all," said Nell with a quick little laugh.

"Get a move on, ladies, or the train's gonna leave without us," said Charles.

The Dansworth family stood on the platform on the Front and waited for the 3:45 train to Huntington. They would have to change trains there for the short trip over the Ohio River into Ironton, Ohio.

Charles was right. Ironton was the perfect remedy for the gloom that hung over the Cole house in Peach Creek. A breeze blew across the Ohio, just enough to blow out the humidity and cool the air. When the train arrived, Charles saw his sister, in a wide-brimmed straw hat waving at him.

Charles smiled and thought to himself, *Alma has always been a party all by herself.* The Dansworth family piled into her big green Packard with camel-colored leather seats.

Alma's big brick house was filled with exuberant bouquets of dahlias and gladiolas and roses of every color. A coconut cake, Charles's favorite, sat on the dining-room buffet under a glass dome. Cab Calloway played on the gramophone in the sitting room. Windows were open wide and the upstairs bedrooms on the north side of the house were cool. Freshly washed sheets smelled like the wind.

It didn't take long for the Dansworth family to become enchanted with their surroundings and their hostess.

Alma was a woman in her forties with short auburn waves framing her face. Folks referred to her as cute. Her green eyes and cupid lips were almost always caught up in an amused expression. She was short like her brother but with soft corners. Alma had never married. She had been teaching high school math for twenty years and counted every student one of her own.

"Aren't you a sight for sore eyes," she exclaimed, as she sliced up the cake and poured lemonade into cut-glass goblets. "My goodness, look at you two girls. You must be Faith; you're the spitting image of your Mama. And Marion, I'd know you anywhere. You've got the Dansworth eyes."

Both sisters were swept up in Alma's bosom in an enormous hug. Then she held them at arm's length and spun them around. "Beautiful, beautiful," she declared.

Next it was Sadie's turn for the Alma inspection.

"And you are just too skinny. I'm going to fatten you up, just you wait, Sadie."

She held on to Charles for a good minute before she scolded him for staying away for so many years.

"Good gracious, brother. To think I've never met these lovely daughters of yours and Faith almost completely grown-up already. Shame on you."

"Couldn't afford to make the trip. You know that, Sis. Still wouldn't be here if our Pa hadn't left me the travel money when he passed."

With that, she served them pimento-cheese sandwiches, bread-and-butter pickles, and coconut cake.

ELEVEN

AND SO BEGAN A BLISSFUL VISIT. Alma pulled out all the stops. She planned a family reunion with all nine of her and Charles's brothers and sisters. There were so many Dansworth cousins that Faith and Marion lost track. Aunt Alma took Sadie and the girls shopping downtown and bought them new hats. At first Sadie was reluctant to take Alma up on her offer, but Alma insisted.

"What fun is it to have all you gals visit if I can't spoil you a little bit? This may be my only chance."

Sadie gave in and chose a refined, understated hat in a gray-blue felt with a pale sky-blue grosgrain ribbon around the brim. Faith picked one made of finely woven golden straw with a green polka-dot bow at the back, which showed off her red ringlets beautifully. "Nell will love it," she said to Marion.

Marion tried on so many hats everyone lost count. "They're all so dreamy, I can't decide," said Marion.

Mama replied with one of her old-time sayings, "Can't fell in a mud hole, and Try pulled him out!"

"Mama, I am trying. It's just that they are all so beautiful."

Finally Aunt Alma said, "I think this is the one!"

It was a pink affair with lots of narrow ribbons and tulle around a wide brim. "Exuberant" is what Alma called it with a chuckle. Marion loved the hat so much she refused to take it off all day. Mother drew the line at bedtime and insisted that Marion take it off to sleep. Reluctantly, Marion placed it next to herself on the nightstand, at the ready for next day's wear.

On Saturday, the whole family packed into Alma's Packard and headed south across the Kentucky line to Dreamland. One of Charles's brothers and sister-in-law and their six kids met them there. Papa bought tickets to the Red Devil, the Whirlwind, and the Chute for all the kids who were old enough for the rides. Uncle Burk treated everyone to cotton candy despite Sadie's protests.

"It's bad for their teeth."

"Oh, come on, Sadie. It's not every day that we're all together like this."

The kids were jumping up and down with such excitement that Sadie said yes once again.

"I think it's time you had some fun, too," said Charles to his wife.

Faith watched as Papa took her mother by the hand and got in line for the Ferris wheel. The carny worker locked the bar across them and up they went. Charles put his arm around Sadie as she looked out into the night. It sparkled with stars and carnival lights. The second time around, the Ferris wheel stopped, and Faith could see her parents swaying at the top. Sadie leaned over and kissed Charles. The kiss was no peck on the lips. Faith was surprised.

Down below, the cousins were sitting on benches next to the Ferris wheel, mouths and fingers covered in sticky spun sugar. By the time Charles and Sadie got back, the crew was ready for a trip down the Chute. Marion was fearless as she slid down the winding tube into a pile of hay. She begged to go again. Papa bought more tickets.

It wasn't until the rides closed down at midnight that the two families found their way back to their cars parked in a field next to Dreamland. The parents covered the children in blankets in the back seats, certain that they would sleep on the hour-long ride back home. They had ridden every ride at least once, their bellies were full of corn dogs and lemonade and cotton candy. Even Marion had gotten to pick her favorite pony on the merry-go-round, music blaring and lights flashing.

With Alma behind the wheel, Papa snored softly, leaning against Sadie's shoulder in the front seat, and Marion dropped off before they were out of the parking lot, but Faith was wide awake. She couldn't get Henry out of her head. It was worse at night. There was a longing she had never felt before, and the kiss on the front porch was all she could think about. She had kissed a few boys in the dark playing spin the bottle, but she had never had a real boyfriend to kiss. This was different. When she thought about Henry and how sure he was kissing her and how right it felt, her insides warmed up in places she had never felt before. It was thrilling and, at the same time, disturbing. She couldn't wait to see him again and yet was afraid to see him. *What will I say? What if he kissed me just because he felt sorry for me? Will he get a girlfriend at Marshall in the fall when I'm back in Seattle? And what about Nell? She clearly likes Henry, too.* Faith was filled with uncertainty and a whole bundle of brand new feelings.

Aunt Alma had another surprise for the girls on Sunday after church.

"Come help me pack us up this picnic basket, girls," she said. "We're all going up in the hills to visit Great Uncle John. I'm bringing lots of extra food for him. He only goes to the store twice a year, and I know how dear he holds apple cake. Charles is filling up a crate with peaches and pears I put up last summer, along with my famous pickled beets and bread-and-butter pickles."

"Why does he only go to the store twice a year," asked Marion, twirling a ribbon on her hat.

It had been on her head since church earlier that morning and wasn't likely to come off any time soon.

"He's a real honest-to-goodness hermit and he has some strange ways, but I know you are going to like him. He's a wonderful storyteller."

Aunt Alma maneuvered the big Packard over ruts as they bounced up and down on the mountain roads with hairpin curves. The passengers slipped and slid into each other with every turn Alma made until they reached an area with a small meadow. Alma slammed on the brake and they lurched to a stop. Papa turned to his girls in the back seat and whispered, "She drives like a madwoman."

"Come on, everyone. We've got a little hike ahead of us and a lot to carry. Everyone grab something."

There wasn't much of a path but Alma knew right where she was going. She had made this trip every summer for years. Finally the family reached a little clearing next to a rock face and a few scruffy trees. The air was much cooler up here, and the view was breathtaking. It was clear enough to see the mighty Ohio River in the far distance. There was a little creek meandering to the side of the rocks where it fell into a small pool in a crevice. Faith noticed him first, sitting on a tree stump beside an opening in the rock face. She was too shy to say anything, but Charles spoke up.

"Uncle John, over here. It's me, Charles." Charles set the crate of canned goods on the ground.

John jumped up, took a few strides on long lean legs, and extended his hand. John was an old man; how old was hard to tell, and when Marion asked him, he said he didn't reckon he paid much attention to such things. Alma guessed he had to be in his mid- to late eighties.

John had a shiny dome, and his clear blue eyes were framed with wrinkles from squinting in the bright sun for so many years. His skin was like leather and a white beard covered the bottom half of his face. John was dressed in a green flannel shirt tucked into patched bib overalls. The soles of his work boots were tied with twine to the leather uppers and they looked like they hadn't left his feet for years.

Marion whispered, "He looks like Santa Claus, Faith."

"Bring me one of them apple cakes, Alma?" said John.

Alma laughed from deep in her belly.

"You old coot. Of course I did. Do you think I'd dare make the hike up here without it? And look at what else I brought, something even better than apple cake. Charles and his lovely wife and daughters."

Sadie said, "Hello, Uncle John. It's been awhile."

"Yep," said John.

He took the crate and carried it deep into the cave and set it down. He motioned them into the cave.

"He's not much of a talker," said Aunt Alma to Faith as they took up the rear. "But he'll warm up in a bit. You just wait."

Marion took Papa's hand and everyone followed into the dark cave. It took Faith a moment or two for her eyes to adjust to the darkness, but when they did, she was surprised at how roomy the interior was. A table made of gnarled branches and a recycled dresser top of some sort stood in the middle of the cave close to the entrance. A couple of stools made of tree stumps served as chairs. A kerosene lantern, a tin cup and plate, and a pitcher all sat atop the table. A bucket of water was on the dirt floor, and a hatchet leaned up against one of the stone walls. Marion spotted the mule first, clear in the back of the cave.

"Who's that, Uncle John?" asked Marion.

"Why, that's Cat," he said.

Faith began to laugh as she noticed the confusion on Marion's face.

"Marion thinks Cat is a cat," said Faith.

"I do not! I know he's a mule," she replied.

"Now there's a story for you," said Uncle John. "I used to have a whole passel of cats. I went up the mountain one day to gather up wood that fell after a big ole windstorm. It was cold as a witch's tit and the cats was all curled up in a heap in the cave tryin' to keep warm. I came back after a while and dumped the kindling out against the cave and was about to cover it with a tarp that had been layin' near the bed. I lifted the tarp up, and sure as can be, there was a whole nest of vipers. They was tryin' to stay warm, too, I reckon. Well, I got the hatchet and went after them. I got most of 'em, but two slithered away before I could chop off their heads."

Marion's eyes were wide as saucers as she held tight to Papa's hand. Faith was too old to hold Papa's hand, but she was just as scared.

"John, you're scaring the girls," said Alma.

"No, no. Don't stop now," said Marion. "I'm not scared."

Everyone laughed, and John resumed the story.

"I went to check on the cats, reached down to give them a scratch behind the ears, and that's when I noticed it."

He paused for dramatic effect. He knew he had Marion and Faith eating out of his hand.

"Noticed what?" asked Faith.

"The cats was all dead. Stiff as starched shirts, poor things. Those copperheads had gotten every one of them."

"So what's that got to do with the mule," asked Charles, trying to change the subject.

"Hold your horses, son," said John. "I'd always called ole mule back there 'Mule,' but after I lost all them cats, I decided to call him 'Cat' in remembrance of them."

This brought more laughter.

"Let's have some lunch on that note," said Alma.

Faith found a quilt, headed out of the cave and into the sunlight, and spread the quilt on the ground under an elm near the stream. It felt good to get out of the dark cave and away from the viper story. John relished the chicken-salad sandwiches, potato salad, lemonade, and the molasses cookies.

He offered to cut everyone a piece of his apple cake but Alma said, "That's all for you. I would be obliged if you would sing for your supper, though."

John jumped up and pulled a harmonica from deep in his pocket. To everyone's amazement and delight, John began to play a lively tune on the harmonica and dance a jig. His boots flew over the grass, and he kicked his heels together. It was clear he was having as much fun performing for the family as they had watching his little show. When he was done and just a little breathless, everyone clapped, and he sat back down.

"Where do you sleep, Uncle John?" asked Marion.

She was full of questions for this curious relative.

"Marion!" said Mama.

John looked Sadie in the eye and said, "Let the girl talk. Askin' questions is how young'uns learn."

"I didn't see your bed. Where do you sleep?"

"Beds and blankets are witched, wee thing. I got Cat to keep me warm. We settle down for the night on a bed of ashes up against the back wall. Suits me fine."

"Why do you live up here all alone?" Marion continued.

Sadie gave her one of those "Hold it right there, Missy" looks.

Marion knew the look and stopped.

Alma said, "We should be heading back pretty soon. We don't want to be on these winding roads after the sun goes down."

Faith heard Charles whisper to Sadie, "Not with that madwoman driving us!"

On the ride home Marion didn't stop talking. She was beside herself with curiosity about her hermit uncle.

"Why does he live up there all by himself, Mama? Doesn't he get lonely? And what does he mean that blankets and beds are witched?"

"He's a hermit, Marion," said Faith. "He likes the way he lives. Isn't that right, Papa?"

"Yes, it is. Being he was raised up in the woods as a boy, I expect this isn't much different than his bringing up. He never had much schooling and he doesn't take to city ways. I think he's uncomfortable around people he doesn't know. He sure does seem to be a happy fellow if you ask me. He's just different from most folks. That's all."

That seemed to satisfy Marion, except she still couldn't get over him sleeping on ashes with a mule. Mama wouldn't even let Tucker Boy, their beagle, on the bed. The idea of infrequent bathing appealed to her, though.

Their week at Aunt Alma's was nearly over, and Mama and Faith were packing things up.

"You've got to come down to Peach Creek for a few days and help us celebrate Kitty's fortieth birthday. It's July 27, and George's sister Elizabeth is throwing a big party. Kitty would love it if you came," she said.

"I wouldn't dream of missing it. Besides, I've fallen in love with my nieces, and I do want to see you all again at least one more time. Marion reminds me a bit of myself when I was her age. And I'd say Faith takes after you. Much more the responsible one. And smart, too. I think you're destined for something big, Faith."

Faith didn't say anything but her heart expanded at the prediction.

Alma took a breath and paused, looking directly at her sister-in-law. "Don't get upset with what I'm about to say. You know I love you. It's just that I worry that you have gotten so thin. It's like the stuffing has been torn out. I want the old Sadie back. This new version is tired and sad looking. It's clear that Becky's death has taken a terrible toll on you."

Sadie turned her back and began folding Marion's dresses intently.

"I'm doing OK. Please don't worry about me."

"Have you been to the cemetery?" asked Alma.

"Why does everyone keep asking me that?"

Alma said, "I'm really not trying to pry, but it's like you have a little dark cloud over your head. I just think you'd feel better if you could make peace with the whole thing. None of it was your fault, Honey."

Charles bounded up the stairs to carry the grips.

"Ready, Ladies?"

Alma insisted on driving them to the station for the trip back to Peach Creek. There were hugs and kisses and promises to see each other on the 27th. The Dansworth family boarded the 10:04 right on time.

The week in Ironton did just what Papa had hoped. Aunt Alma could cheer up a roomful of sad sacks without even trying. And the Fourth of July is just a week away, Faith thought.

PART TWO

JULY 1932
THE GRAND JURY

IT WAS GLORIOUS TO WALK down Main Street now. The peach trees were lush with leaves, providing ample shade for the citizens of Peach Creek, and the golf ball-sized peaches were so abundant that some of the neighbors took to thinning them out a bit.

TWELVE

By the time the Dansworth family returned from Ohio, Nell had almost completely recovered. The swelling in her ankle was gone, and Doc Howard had declared her mended. All that remained of the bite was a small scab and a little bit of bruising around the ankle. Nell greeted Faith on her return with a hug and a request to go to Logan that afternoon for a flapper Coke at the five-and-dime. "Look! I finished," she declared, holding up the prettiest pink tulle dress.

"It's gorgeous, Nell!" said Faith. "And I haven't even finished the skirt on my dress. I'm going to have to work like a fiend to get it done in time for the fete."

Aunt Kitty's party was only three weeks away.

"Do you think Henry will be at the party?"

"I'm sure he was invited along with his parents, but I doubt any of them will come, what with Mr. Thompson arrested for murder and all. And Mama says Mrs. Thompson is nowhere to be seen. I guess she doesn't even come down to eat. And the twins are gone for the rest of the summer staying with their grandparents in Huntington. I know I wouldn't be able to show my face if, gosh forbid, my daddy did something like that."

"Oh, for goodness sake, the grand jury hasn't even met yet."

"Faith, you haven't read the paper for a week. There was a whole lot of nasty business going on over there in Logan. Papa'd kill me if he knew I'd been keeping up with the news in the *Tribune*. It wasn't just Mr. Thompson who was having an affair with that woman. According to the *Tribune*, she had a list of sixteen other men she was sleeping with. Can you believe it?" Nell paused to take a breath and see what effect this juicy tidbit had on Faith and then continued. "Seems there's a key club, the Amore Club, right above the five-and-dime on Main Street. A lot of bad stuff goes on at night up there. I don't know how Henry or his mom can stand it. It's horrible."

Faith took a deep breath. She really hadn't thought about the murder while at Aunt Alma's. She felt her innards tighten. Faith could see that all this murder business was titillating to Nell, but for her it was simply disturbing and hard to believe.

"Where's the *Tribune?* I want to read it for myself. I can't believe it's true. After all, Mrs. Gannon was married and your mom said she was nice. How did she manage to have all these relations?"

"She was nice all right, a little too nice. Maybe it all happened at the key club, I don't know," Nell said. "Mama threw the papers in the trash, but I pulled them out when she left the kitchen 'cause I knew you'd want to read them. They're under the bed. Let's go on up and you can read them for yourself, if you don't believe me."

The two cousins were on their way to the bedroom when a piercing shriek shot through the house. "Mama, Papa," wailed Marion, slamming the screen door.

Nell and Faith turned and ran down the stairs. Sadie and Kitty came running from the kitchen and Charles put down his tools and rushed in the house. Everyone was there except Rusty. He stood alone in a corner on the front porch, head down.

"Settle down, Marion," said Mother. "What is all this screaming about?"

"He let him out. I told him not to. He promised. I hate him!"

All this came out in short bursts between the sobs. Marion's cheeks were on fire and her whole body was shaking.

"Who let who out?" said Papa.

Marion looked out the screen door and pointed.

"Rusty! He let Broadway out of his box and now he's gone," she cried.

Marion rushed to the door, fists up, but Charles grabbed her by the arm.

"Hold on there. You leave your cousin alone. Settle down right now, Marion Dorothy Dansworth."

Both Faith and Marion knew that tone. They didn't hear it often but when they did, they knew that Papa meant business and there might be a hairbrush to their backsides if they didn't obey. Marion sucked in air and quit resisting her father's grip.

Everyone looked out on the porch and saw poor Rusty cowering in the corner. He looked genuinely afraid of Marion.

"I didn't mean to. Broadway just hopped out when I was offering him a caterpillar," he said, still on the other side of the screen door. "I tried to catch him, but he took off in the raspberry patch and he got away."

Kitty said, trying to hold back a laugh, "You come in here, young man. When did this happen and why didn't you tell me? Tell your cousin you are sorry."

There was no convincing Marion that Broadway was much happier out in the countryside than living in a cardboard box. She grudgingly accepted Rusty's apology only because she knew Papa would give her a spanking if she didn't. Then she stomped through the kitchen and outside to look for Broadway.

"It's OK, Rusty. We all know it was an accident and that Broadway is far happier now," said Charles. "I think I'd stay clear of Marion for now if I were you."

Rusty put up no argument.

Faith and Nell headed upstairs for the second time.

Nell pulled the *Tribune* from under the bed. All the things Nell said were true. Bart Strout was the lead reporter for the *Logan Tribune* and his byline was all over the newspaper. One article gave a more detailed report of the blood and other evidence. Strout reported that Sidney was the one who drove the Ford with the dogs in the back seat. That's where the sheriff's deputies found blood. According to the paper, Sidney lived in the Thompsons' attic and washed up in their basement. He did odd jobs around the house, but mostly he took care of the hunting dogs, a pack of beagles trained to hunt foxes, a fact which Faith already knew.

"I met those dogs when Sidney brought Marion home. I just can't believe Sidney was involved in the murder."

Faith went back to the article; Mr. Thompson had a small hunting cabin up Holden Road on Trace Mountain, and Sidney drove the dogs up in the Ford whenever there was a hunt. They called the Ford the "dog car."

"Them dogs was always fightin' in the back, and I didn't never have time to hose down the tarp," Sidney was quoted. But that didn't explain the bloody rags in the basement along with a straight razor. Things didn't look good for Sidney or for Henry's dad.

Another front-page column was headlined "Amour Club Has Many Prominent Members." It went on to explain how the pillars of society in Logan County had keys to this club above the five-and-dime.

"Wouldn't you love to get your hands on the list of members?" said Nell.

Faith was too engrossed in the paper to even notice what Nell said. She thought of Henry and wondered how he was dealing with all of this horrible news.

"Maybe I'll bake Henry some gingersnaps," said Faith out loud, although she wasn't really speaking to Nell.

"I don't think cookies are going to help," said Nell. "If I was Henry, I'd get out of town like his little sisters did. The Thompsons are treated like pariahs. Henry's teammates don't even come around anymore."

"But that's just not fair. He didn't do anything."

"No, but according to the paper, his daddy was busy doin' all sorts of stuff. And here he is, chairman of the city council, passing ordinances about loitering and drunkenness, and he's upstairs doing way more than that," said Nell. "Now put that paper down. I've got a plan. I'm about to die of cabin fever and I feel fit as a fiddle. Let's sneak out later and go down to Peck's Mill. I heard that a bunch of kids are meeting down there at midnight to swim. Let's go."

"I don't know, Nell. Maybe we shouldn't."

"Oh, come on," said Nell, dragging out each word.

Not wanting to be a prude, Faith agreed to the plan.

About eleven fifteen, after making sure the house was fast asleep, Nell and Faith pulled their bathing suits on, grabbed a couple of towels, and tiptoed down the stairs. The temperature hadn't dropped all day, and a dip in the Guyandotte River did sound inviting. The girls rode their bikes in the dark to the Mill. Faith had never done anything like this before, and the thrill of it set her heart racing. When they arrived, there were a dozen teenagers already in the water. Nell ran to the bank and shouted to her friends. Faith scanned the group, hoping to see Henry. He wasn't there.

"Come on in, Faith," shouted Nell, already atop an inner tube with some boy. It was too dark for Faith to recognize who it was.

The cool water was great, and Faith floated on her back for a long time. The night sky was dazzling. She was lost in thoughts of Henry, the picture show, his smile, the wink, the kiss on the front porch. She floated closer to Nell and realized that Nell was with Walter.

"Hey, Faith, glad you came," he said to her.

"Where's Henry? Did you tell him?" asked Faith.

Walter didn't answer, but it was clear he hadn't. Faith wasn't paying attention to the other kids until she heard a boy talking.

"The Klan will string that nigger up if the courts don't. My daddy said there's no way in hell Sidney'll get away with it."

Another voice, a boy's, responded, "The Klan's gonna be in back of the courtroom every day of the trial, whenever Sidney is around. My pa says they'll stare him down and make him squirm. You don't mess with a white woman and get away with it."

A shiver went through Faith. She stopped swimming and treaded water, hoping to see who the boys were who were talking. She didn't recognize them. She began to tremble. The voices started up again.

"I say let's go up to Trace Mountain and poke around where they found the body. I brought a flashlight."

"What do you think we'll find?"

"Who cares? Let's go."

The boys swam away from her. She watched as five teenage boys went ashore, dried themselves off, and climbed into a blue pickup truck. The tires squealed as they peeled off.

Maybe she was just chilled from the swim, but she couldn't stop shaking. She pulled herself up on the riverbank and found her towel draped over her bike. As she was drying off, Nell shouted to her, "Hey, cousin, how come you're getting out?"

Faith could just make out Nell's and Walter's silhouettes out in the middle of the river.

"I'm cold," Faith hollered back.

Nell left Walter and swam ashore.

"You're looking for Henry, aren't you?"

"All your friends are here, so where's Henry?" asked Faith.

Nell said, "We decided not to tell him that we were meeting down here."

"Why not?"

"Oh, come on. He'd just put a wet blanket on everything. Besides, he probably wouldn't come anyway," said Nell. "Please come on back in."

Faith looked at the kids left splashing around in the river and on the shore wrapped in towels and blankets. A group of boys was gathered on the bank drying off, and a few couples were necking in the moonlight.

I feel like a fifth wheel, a fat fifth wheel, Faith thought. She looked at Nell and began squeezing her damp feet into her shoes.

"I'm going back. Stay if you want. I know the way home."

She swung her leg over the bike and began pedaling slowly, feeling very alone and out of place.

"Come on, Faith. Just a little while."

Faith could hear Walter calling Nell's name through the night air. Faith kept riding.

The next day, Sadie asked Charles, "Can you go into Logan to the pharmacy and pick up some aspirin? Kitty's out, and so am I. My headaches are coming back, and I want to be prepared. And while you're in town, stop at Leonetti's Bakery and bring some donuts home. I've got a craving."

"Can I come with you, Papa?" asked Faith.

She hadn't spent much time with her father since they had gotten back from Ironton. It was nice to be alone with him for the fifteen-minute ride to town, bumping along in Uncle George's old pickup truck.

"Why so glum, Sweet Pea?" said Charles.

"I don't know. Maybe I'm just missing my friends back home."

Charles turned his head toward his daughter. This was more than a little case of homesickness.

"You can tell your pa."

Faith sighed. "It's nothing. I'm a little tired, I guess."

"How 'bout we grab some lunch at the five-and-dime after I pick up Ma's pills?" said Charles.

Charles and Faith found two stools at the end of the counter. Faith ordered a cold plate and Charles a meatloaf sandwich. They both had coffee. They sat without talking for a while.

Finally Faith blurted out, "I heard some boys talking about the Klan and stringing up that colored man who found Marion. Papa, he seemed like such a nice fellow. He was very gentle with Marion, and he was so shy."

She rolled up her sleeves, in hopes it would help her cool off a bit. "Would the Klan really kill him?"

Charles was quiet for a while. Faith could tell her papa didn't want to get into the topic, but he took a big breath and began.

"The Klan is a fraternal order, a little like the Elks or the Odd Fellows. The difference is that the membership's a secret. They do some good things like supporting better schools for poor whites, but they do more harm, in my opinion."

The coffee arrived. Faith added three spoonsful of sugar to hers. Papa took his black or "barefoot" as it was called in West Virginia. Faith took a sip from her cup and proceeded.

"They do bad things to the colored, don't they?" said Faith.

"That's true. They don't like race mixing."

Papa paused, wondering how much he should tell his daughter.

"Will they hang Sidney?" asked Faith in a soft voice.

"They might. His hands are all bloodied up in the killing."

When the waitress put their lunches in front of them, neither had much of an appetite.

Picking at her chicken salad, Faith said, "Do we know anybody in the Klan, Papa? Uncle George isn't a member, is he?"

"Absolutely not! He's a union man and the Klan hates the unions, communists, and Catholics along with Negroes."

Faith thought about what Papa had told her. She knew there was much more he hadn't said. She barely said a word on the ride home.

As they were driving by the Front at the switching station outside Peach Creek, Charles said, "By the way, when did you hear those boys talking? I don't remember you being with any kids since we got back."

Darn! There go my ears again, Faith thought.

She could feel the heat and knew she could blow Nell's secret. She wasn't good at lying.

"I don't remember, exactly. The other day, I guess."

Faith was glad that Papa didn't press her any further. Anyway, her ears were a dead giveaway.

THIRTEEN

THE HOUSE WAS ABUZZ WITH Fourth of July plans. Kitty had jobs assigned to everyone in the household in anticipation of Tuesday's big parade and picnic in Peach Creek.

"Kitty has this house and everyone in it running like a fine-tuned army platoon," said Sadie to her daughter. "This is her favorite holiday, ever better than Christmas. Just get out of her way and let her have her fun."

Faith did just that, making a mental note of the details of the day as they unfolded.

Rusty convinced his mother that he needed red, white, and blue crepe paper to decorate his two-wheel bike. Marion got into the act and forgave her cousin over the Broadway affair so she could help decorate Nell's old bike and be in her first-ever parade. Rusty showed Marion how to take a playing card and attach it to the spokes of the back wheel with a clothespin so that it made the best clacking noise.

"Almost like it's motorized," said Rusty.

Faith was too old for such childish ventures, but secretly she wished that she could decorate a bike and ride through town. Instead, she helped Nell decorate the front porch, wrapping the red, white, and blue crepe paper round and round the white pillars. Nell climbed up on the porch railing to hang Old Glory straight down from the front gutter. She was so much taller than Faith that she could reach to the top of the gutter without even stretching. *What I'd give for those legs*, Faith thought.

They were giving out little flags at the bank, so Sadie and Kitty went twice with all the children to get enough for everyone. Marion taped hers to the basket of her bike, the older girls planted a couple in with the pots of geraniums and kept out enough to wave from the porch the day of the parade.

Kitty volunteered the men without them knowing, but Faith could tell that they were both glad to get out from underfoot of the womenfolk. Charles and George worked most of Saturday morning at the city park, building a makeshift stage out of lumber donated by the lumberyard. The stage would be used for the band and the politicians giving speeches after the parade. When the stage was built, all the men went to the Peach Pit and cooled down with a beer.

Early every morning the last couple of days the oven was heated up so breads and pies and cookies could bake before the heat of the day. Charles splurged and bought a huge watermelon at the Piggly Wiggly along with a big bag of lemons to make a gallon of lemonade. On Monday, Kitty baked a ham. Macaroni noodles cooked in a large pot on the back of the stove and then were drained and cooled. Kitty chopped sweet pickles and onions and celery and stirred it all together with mayonnaise into a macaroni salad.

"Looks like we're feeding the whole gosh-damn town," said George, on the morning of the Fourth.

"Watch your language," said Kitty, pecking him on the cheek. "Did you get two blocks of ice? We've got to keep all this food and drink cool for the picnic."

He kissed her back. "Yes, ma'am."

On the Fourth of July Faith pulled back the lace curtains in the sitting room to see how the porch decorations looked. Clouds hung heavy, and the air was so thick it was hard to breathe.

"All that work and now it looks like the parade will be rained out," said Sadie.

"Let's hope those clouds open up and it clears out by parade time," said Kitty. "Say a little prayer to the Lord."

She had no sooner said that than lightning lit up the holler, and within just a few seconds thunder rolled across the hills, and the rain came down in sideways sheets.

"I can't believe how hard it rains here," said Faith.

"How does it rain in Seattle?" asked Aunt Kitty.

"Mostly it just drizzles all winter long. It hardly ever rains much in the summer, but I don't remember it ever raining this hard," said Faith.

Rivulets were flowing down their street, and the puddles were rapidly growing into ponds. Marion and Rusty stood on the couch and looked out through the lace curtains, watching the crepe paper decorations turn soggy and bleed red and blue over the white pillars.

"Our bikes!" yelled Rusty, as he raced for the sidewalk.

It was too late. The streamers were a soggy mess. He pulled his bike up on the covered porch. Marion came racing out after him. They looked at each other, sharing the disappointment.

Faith saw the two of them and their sad-sack faces and called them inside.

"Maybe Aunt Kitty is right and everything will dry out in time for the parade. Let's cross our fingers."

She handed them each a sugar cookie she had frosted in red and white stripes. That seemed to help a little.

Aunt Kitty was indeed right. As quick as it came, the rain stopped, and the sun came out. The air was washed clean. In no time the heat of the day dried everything out. However, the crepe paper didn't quite recover. It shriveled up and was faded to a pastel pink and blue.

"The bikes are ruined," wailed Rusty.

But they were good enough according to Marion, who had never been in a parade before and was determined not to miss this one.

"Come on, Rusty." said Faith. "I'll give both of you a couple of my red-and-blue hair ribbons for the handle bars, and they will look even better than they did before."

When it was time for the parade to begin, Charles, Sadie and Faith, and George, Kitty and Nell sat on the porch steps under bright skies that gave no hint of the morning cloudburst. Marion and Rusty rode their bikes, now bedecked with ribbons, faded streaked crepe-paper streamers, and new playing cards, clattering down to the end of Main Street. They joined the lineup in the elementary school play yard with most every other kid from Peach Creek. The Independent Order of Odd Fellows band was warming up on the makeshift grandstand in the park two blocks away, and the Sousa marches drifted down the street and mixed with the Peach Creek High School band also lining up at the school yard.

"Anyone wants some lemonade," said Kitty, "better get a glass now, because I think the parade's about to begin."

Horses and riders pranced down the street doing tricks and turns right in front of the Coles' porch. Then came the politicians in cars with campaign signs and Rebel flags taped to the sides, horns honking. The high school band, led by the drum major in a tall feathered hat and girls twirling batons and tossing them high in the air with surprisingly few mishaps, came next. Everyone on the porch stood when the flag passed, held high by the Boy Scouts. Next came the Shriners all decked out in crazy clown suits with huge wigs and big red noses, tossing handfuls of candy to the bystanders. But the highlight for the Coles and Dansworths was when the thirty or so neighbor children on bikes rode past. Cards clicked and clattered and bicycle bells rang on every bike.

"Here they come," said Sadie. Marion rode by, did a big circle in front of the porch, and grinned from ear to ear, waving at her family. "Look at her, Charles," said Sadie. "She is having the time of her life."

Rusty rode with all the boys and popped a wheelie as he passed by. The family cheered wildly. Nell put two fingers to her lips and gave her brother a whistle that could be heard over in the next holler. Rusty gave her a thumbs-up.

Kids scattered out on the street gathering up candy thrown by the volunteer firemen on the fire truck.

The last band that followed the fire truck was the Logan County High School Panthers, the only Negro high school around. Though the band was small and the uniforms were just simple black trousers with white shirts, they had the crowd clapping and stomping their feet with their jazzy music and high-stepping marches.

"Well, I think that's it," said George. "The colored kids are always the last band, and it looks like the shit crew is right behind."

Kitty gave her husband a look with eyebrows raised as the shovel brigade came by scooping up horse manure.

It struck Faith that her uncle had made that statement without a note of awareness that it was just what it was. Negroes always came last.

After the parade the two families headed to the city park and ball field, loaded down with balls and bats, tablecloths, food, and a big washtub resting on Rusty's old wagon which was filled with ice, a gallon jug of lemonade, and one huge watermelon.

"Let's try and get a table with a little shade," said Charles.

They found a perfect spot under an old dogwood close to the horseshoe pit. Nell and Faith were spreading the tablecloth over the wooden table when Nell spotted Henry walking all alone toward the horseshoe pit.

"Hey, Faith, look who's coming. Henry, over here," waved Nell.

Henry looked up and waved in their general direction. Faith's heart skipped a beat as she waved back, willing her ears to not pink up.

"Let's go!" said Nell, as she sprinted on her long legs in Henry's direction.

Seeing Henry all alone tugged at Faith. Looking around the park, Faith saw groups of revelers enjoying the festivities. People were laughing, filling their plates with picnic food, and engaging in games and conversation. She resolved to make Henry feel a part of things. Nell had the same idea.

"Henry, come join us. We've set up over there under the dogwood tree," said Nell. "And we've got more food and lemonade than we know what to do with."

"Is your family coming?" asked Nell, knowing full well that they wouldn't dare show their faces. The grand jury planned to meet in a couple of weeks to determine whether or not to charge Henry's father and his handyman with the murder of Gloria Gannon.

"No, I just decided to come over and maybe join a ball game or something."

Just then the band struck up a loud and lively rendition of "It's a Grand Ole Flag."

"Must be time for the mayor's speech. We can count on an hour of political dribble," said Nell, linking her arm in Henry's. "Let's get some of Mama's ham and macaroni salad."

"You enjoying yourself, Faith?" asked Henry, linking his other arm with Faith's. Nell gave Faith a withering look as the three of them headed for the food. Kitty piled Henry's plate with picnic food. Charles moved over on the bench. "Have a seat, Henry. Good to see you."

"Want to play catch, Henry?" asked Rusty tossing a ball in and out of a worn-out mitt.

"Sure, but just for a bit. I've got something I need to take care of. Let me finish my plate first. This is mighty fine food."

"What do you need to take care of on the Fourth of July, for goodness sake?" asked Faith.

Henry was already tossing the ball to Rusty, gently at first, until he realized what a strong arm Rusty had for a boy of nine.

"Hang on, Faith. I'll tell you when we're finished."

Rusty threw the ball hard and even got a little spin on it.

"OK, Buddy. That's it for now. I've gotta run."

With that Rusty ran over to watch his dad and some of the other men tossing horseshoes. Seemed no one was interested in the speeches at the bandstand. Faith could hear faint applause over the laughter and talking in other parts of the park. It was hard to compete with baseball, horseshoes, and food.

Kitty and Sadie left to sit with women friends from the First Baptist Church, listening to the band music between the speeches, and Marion was at the swings.

"There's Walter," said Nell, pointing to a picnic table nearby. "Let's all go over."

"In a minute, Nell," said Faith.

"Come on, Henry," said Nell, as she took Henry's hand.

Henry gently pulled his hand back and looked Nell squarely in the eye. "I need to tell Faith something. It won't take long." He turned and sat at the table.

Nell looked back over her shoulder at the two of them sitting side by side. She had a surprised look on her face, straightened her back, and kept walking.

"Why are you in such a hurry, and what's so urgent that you have to rush off on the Fourth of July?" Faith asked Henry.

"I only have my dad's car until four o'clock. I'm going up to Trace Mountain to see the spot where Mrs. Gannon's body was dumped," said Henry. "No one'll be up there today so I'll be able to poke around without being bothered."

"What do you think you'll find?" asked Faith.

Henry shrugged. "I don't know. Maybe something the deputies missed.

"I'm coming with you," said Faith.

"Are you sure you want to go up there?" asked Henry.

He had a determined look on his face, and Faith was certain he would go up there with or without her.

"Absolutely."

They walked to the big green Buick without stopping at Walter's table. *I'm going to hear about this*, thought Faith.

It was beautiful up top the mountain. They could hear the birds singing as they got out of Mr. Thompson's shiny and expensive car. The air was at least ten degrees cooler and everything felt washed clean from the morning downpour. The alder leaves still held droplets of rain. They seemed to whisper as if they were holding secrets.

"Hold my hand," said Henry.

He held out his hand to Faith and she grabbed hold. Henry slowly led her up the steep mining road, pushing back the tall damp bushes for Faith. After about twenty yards Henry stopped.

"This must be the place. Look how the brush is all trampled down."

He pointed to a spot down the side of the hill off to the right of the road. It was covered in blackberry vines and huckleberry bushes. Many of the branches were bent or broken.

"Maybe I'll find something."

Faith couldn't bring herself to tell him about the boys, many of them his friends, who had come exploring up here the night they all went swimming without him. But it was clear from the condition of the brush that more than the sheriff's deputies had been here.

"What can we possibly find after all this time? It's been a whole month since that Butler boy found the body," said Faith. "I don't think we should climb down there. It's so steep and it's covered in sticker bushes."

Henry put one foot down the slope to test this footing, looked back at her, and kept going.

"You can stay here if you want, but I'm going down."

That was all the challenge she needed. Faith pulled up her skirt and petticoat and held them with one hand as she grabbed a branch and headed down after Henry. She hadn't gone more than a few feet when her foot caught on a bramble and she slipped on the wet soil.

"Ouch!"

Henry turned and saw Faith on the ground in a small clearing. He scrambled up to where she was lying. Her left foot was turned in at an awkward angle.

"Are you OK?"

She had pulled herself to a sitting position and was trying to stand.

"I don't know. I'm such a klutz."

Henry reached down and put his arm around her waist to lift her up. His hand brushed against her breast hidden under three layers of clothes. A shiver ran through Faith. It was wonderful and terrifying all at the same time.

Faith caught her breath. Henry offered his hand, and together they managed to get Faith to a standing position. And then Henry kissed her. She kissed him back.

Faith grabbed a sapling behind her for balance, and as she did she saw something blue peeking from under the forest's fallen debris.

"Henry, stop. I think I found something."

Faith stirred the leaves behind her with her good foot. A shoe appeared, muddy but made of a fine blue leather, a woman's high heeled shoe with a strap across that closed with a brass button shaped like a teardrop.

"Oh, my goodness! I think I found Gloria's shoe," said Faith, holding up the treasure.

Henry straightened himself and took the shoe in his hand. "I think you're right."

"What are you going to do with it?' asked Faith.

She was aware that Henry was as discombobulated by what had just happened as she was. Faith also had the feeling that Henry was as relieved as she was that finding the shoe was a good distraction. Faith was feeling things she didn't know what to do with. She suspected that Henry had similar feelings. His cheeks were flushed and he wouldn't look her in the eye.

Faith took a step to turn around. "Ow. I might have I twisted my ankle a bit," said Faith. "I'm sorry, Henry."

"It's OK, but we better go. You're going to need to put ice on that ankle before it swells up" said Henry. "Can you get to the car if I help you? Maybe you can hop on one foot once we get up the hill."

With that he held her around her waist again, but this time he was all business. Faith put her arms around Henry's neck as he half carried, half dragged her up the muddy hill with the blue shoe still in his hand.

When they reached the top, Faith did her best to straighten her muddy clothes and then hopped the few yards to the car.

"What are you going to do with the shoe?" she asked again as she eased into the front seat.

"I don't know. What do you think?"

Faith thought for a moment. It was good to be focusing on something other than Henry's hands on her body. She looked over at Henry who was staring straight ahead. She could tell that he didn't know what to say to her, either. They rode in silence down the winding mining road with the mud-coated shoe on the seat between them.

"OK, here's what I think you should do," said Faith finally. "First, I don't think we should tell anyone until we have time to really think this through. And second, I think I should keep the shoe with me. What if your mom or dad found it, or worse yet, the sheriff? I can hide it in my grip. It's just stuffed in the back of Nell's closet till we have to pack up for home. We can decide later."

"Oh, I haven't thought about you leaving."

Henry reached across the seat and touched her hand.

"We don't have to think about that now. It's a long way off and we've got more important things to worry about right now," said Faith.

'I hate that you'll be involved," said Henry, "but I guess you're right. Are you sure you're OK with hiding it?"

"Of course. And besides, we don't even know if it really is Gloria's shoe. How do you think the sheriff missed it?"

Henry kept his eyes on the steep twisty road and said, "I suspect the cloudburst this morning washed a lot of mud down the bank and uncovered the shoe. I'm just not sure how a shoe is going to help Dad."

Faith didn't say what she was thinking: that it didn't look like anything could save Henry's father short of an out-and-out confession by someone else, and that didn't seem likely.

It was good to have the thirty-minute drive home to decompress. Faith reached down to rub her ankle, which was beginning to swell.

"We'd better get some ice on that," said Henry, as they reached Peach Creek. "I'll park the car in the alley behind the Coles'. Hopefully everyone is still at the picnic."

Faith said a little prayer to herself. *Please Lord, let everyone still be at the park.*

Henry helped Faith up the back steps and chipped off some ice from the block still in the icebox. He wrapped the ice in a dish towel, set Faith down on a kitchen chair, and instructed her to put her foot up on another chair.

"I'm fine, Henry. You go find my grip and put the shoe in it. It's the room at the top of the stairs. It's way in the back of the closet, kind of beige with trees and houses woven in it. Wrap it in some newspaper. Hurry in case someone decides to come home early."

With the shoe secreted away and twenty minutes of ice treatment, mud and dirt washed off skin and clothing as much as possible, Faith and Henry got back in the car and drove the two blocks to the park. Things were just as Faith had hoped, with one exception.

Marion rushed up to them and shouted, "Where have you two been? We've been looking for you everywhere."

She looked them both up and down and asked, "Why is your face all red? Your backside is all muddy."

Faith was furious and her ears were hot again.

"It's none of your business. I fell, if you must know, Miss Busybody. Go find someone else to play with and leave us alone."

Startled, Marion looked up at her big sister and turned on her heel.

"I'm gonna tell Papa that you're back, and he's gonna want to know where you've been, so there."

Henry looked over toward the ball field and then at the women at the table.

"I think it's best that I take off. I have a feeling there is no shutting Marion up."

"Maybe you're right. I can handle Papa. It's Mother I'm worried about. Hopefully she's having so much fun she's forgotten all about me."

Henry nodded and turned to walk away, but he stopped, looked directly at Faith, and said, "I'm glad you came with me."

He was out of sight before Faith could think of what to say back.

Mama and Papa did want to know where Faith had been, just as Marion had predicted. But they didn't seem upset even though her explanation was more than a little vague.

"Henry asked me to walk up Peach Creek Road to show me where the fish were running. He said they were late this year. And then I fell and twisted my ankle."

Papa even helped Faith home before the rest of the family, noting that her ankle was darned near as big as a cantaloupe.

"You go on back, Papa. I'll keep my foot up and put more ice on it." Papa was already wrapping up some large ice chips in a towel. "You sure, Sweet Pea?" said her father. "I'd just as soon sit here with you."

"No, Papa. You go on and be with everyone."

Faith was happy to have the big old blue house to herself that night. She watched the fireworks from the bedroom window. They were beautiful but no match for the ones up on Trace Mountain that afternoon. She was grateful to have this time alone to think about all that had happened during the day and what it meant for her. There were the feelings that were getting stronger for Henry, and there was the shoe. Was it really Gloria Gannon's? What were the implications for Henry and his family? Would he, should he, turn the shoe in to the police? Faith didn't have any answers, but she did know that this Fourth of July was already burned in her memory.

FOURTEEN

A QUIET WEEK FOLLOWED WITHOUT any word from Henry. Faith woke each morning hoping that this would be the day Henry dropped by, and every night she was disappointed. Her ankle was still tender, but she managed to avoid most of the questions about it and her absence midday at the picnic. The family seemed satisfied that she had simply tripped and twisted her ankle and gotten her backside muddy in the process. Everyone except Marion and Nell, that is.

"I just know there's something you're not telling us," said Nell.

"I already told you guys, and I'm just not going over it again," said Faith.

"Don't worry. I'll get it out of you sooner or later," said Nell.

Technically it's not a lie, thought Faith. *It's just not the whole truth. Why do I feel so guilty?*

When Sunday came, Faith tore through the closet trying on outfits and flinging them in a heap on the floor. She finally settled on a pale-yellow dress with a full skirt. It tied at the back of the waist with a deeper-yellow grosgrain ribbon. The preacher had asked Faith to play the piano this morning. Faith thought the combination of her new summer straw hat from Aunt Alma and the bow at her back with the full skirt draped over the piano bench would be particularly pretty.

"What's going on?" said Nell. "You're running around like a chicken with your head cut off. I bet it's all for Henry."

Faith didn't bother to answer the question.

"Hurry up, Faith," yelled Marion from the bottom of the stairs. "We're all waiting on you."

Faith glanced in the mirror, still not completely satisfied with her looks, but she straightened her hat and ran down the stairs.

At Logan Baptist, Preacher Corn revved up for a long sermon. Marion pulled at the ribbons on her wonderful hat as he pounded on the lectern and admonished his congregation to be pure of heart, quoting the Bible: "'So you also outwardly appear righteous to others, but within you are full of hypocrisy and lawlessness' (Matthew 23: 28). Look into your hearts, dear friends. Are you who you present to your family and neighbors? The Lord knows your heart and soul. He will not be deceived."

Dear God, he's talking about me.

Faith's mind raced without her permission over what happened on Trace Mountain on the Fourth of July. It was a common remembrance now, one that immediately brought back the warm but disturbing feelings inside of her. Feelings she couldn't talk about, even to Nell.

Not in church, Faith admonished herself.

"Let's stand and sing God's praises as we open our hymnals to number 28, 'A Mighty Fortress.' Miss Dansworth?"

Faith was jolted back to the present when she heard her name. She quickly stood up and smoothed her skirt, glancing at the congregation. She didn't see Henry's face anywhere. Faith willed her mind to still, asked Jesus for forgiveness, spread her skirt carefully over the piano bench, and played and sang with unusual gusto. It was good to focus on the music.

She didn't see Henry until the preacher finally released his flock. Nell spotted him, too, and walked briskly to catch up to him. He was alone once again.

Henry stopped and let Nell catch up. Faith hung back a bit. She needed time to let her ears calm down and plan what she would say to him that didn't make her sound like a fool. She finally caught up when a woman in a blue suit with a little purple hat perched atop her head like a bird barged past her and stood squarely in front of Henry at the back of the church.

"Good morning, Henry. We've missed your family. I haven't seen Hazel all month. Everything all right?"

Faith stared at her in disbelief. Did this woman really not know about the murder and that Mrs. Thompson's husband was accused of killing Gloria Gannon? Or did she just want to embarrass Henry? Either way, it was cruel, and Faith didn't need any time to compose her words now.

"How dare you! Why are you asking Henry such a thing? And right here in church. You know perfectly well why Henry's mother isn't here." said Faith in a voice much too loud.

Sadie flew up behind Faith, grabbed her by the elbow, and steered her away from Henry and the woman. Nell just stood with her mouth open looking at Faith.

Sadie was the one with a red face now. "Faith, what are you thinking? You can't speak to people like that."

"But Mother . . ."

"Hush up. You go over there and apologize to that woman right this instant and then get in the car."

Faith knew this was not the time to argue with her mother, so she slid over to the woman and muttered a half-hearted apology. Henry was gone and Nell was standing at the church door waiting for her.

"I can't believe you just did that," said Nell.

"She had it coming," said Faith, still full of rage.

Kitty and George had the younger two in tow as both families walked to the car parked half a block down Stratton. Everyone squeezed into the car. Faith was still fuming inside, not sure if she was madder at the woman or her own mother. No one spoke for the entire ride back to Peach Creek.

As soon as the car was parked, Faith opened the door, saying in a loud voice to no one in particular, "She was a hateful woman, and I'm not sorry for what I said. She was deliberately mean to Henry, and she deserved it." She slammed the car door before Marion could even get out.

With that she ran into the house, up the stairs and flung herself on her bed, beating her clenched fists on the pillow. Nell followed. "Faith, I understand why you are so darn mad, but did it occur to you that you might have embarrassed Henry more by coming to his defense?"

"But I'm the only one who ever sticks up for him."

"Maybe he doesn't want you to."

FIFTEEN

It didn't take long before Logan County citizens had lots more to buzz about. The grand jury convened the third week in July. They were in session for the whole week but didn't get to the Gannon murder until Friday. The decision was swift.

The *Logan Tribune* printed a special edition the day the grand jury ruling was announced. The paper sold out within an hour. Charles got one of the last copies. He drove in to Logan to buy fence posts and chicken wire at the lumberyard, then picked up a paper and headed to Leonetti's to read it. The chickens had found a way through the rickety fence and had literally been flying the coop to strut up and down the back alley. Charles needed to have something to keep himself busy and the fence was just the ticket. He settled in at Leonetti's with a cup of coffee and a donut and spread the paper on the counter in front of him. Charles loved this place. The smell of yeasty breads baking in the old ovens in the back of the bakery was intoxicating, and Mr. Leonetti made a really strong cup of coffee, not Kitty's watered-down Yuban.

Charles took a slow sip from his mug. *Nothin' like that first sip in the morning. It's one of life's simple pleasures,* he thought.

He looked at the headline on the front page of the *Tribune*. It screamed what everyone in the county knew would happen: "Sidney Williams Indicted for the Murder of Gloria Gannon—Robert Thompson Freed." According to Bart Strout's byline, Sidney claimed he was having relations with Gloria, too. The blood from the Ford came back from the laboratory in Charleston positive for human blood, so that whole story about the dogs fighting was just a cover. And Sidney had been seen up Trace Mountain early on the morning she went missing.

What's his motive? I can see why Bill Gannon would kill his wife, or any of the sixteen men who were on Gloria's list of boyfriends, or even Hazel Thompson. A woman scorned and all that. But Sidney? *It doesn't smell right,* he thought.

Charles looked up from the paper and saw Ralph Cole, George's brother. "Morning, Charles. Mind if I join you?"

"Pull up a chair," said Charles. "What are you up to?"

"Just finished up an early morning meeting with the union reps up at Holden 2 about the mine cave-in a couple a weeks ago," continued Ralph. "There're a lot of riled-up folks up there. We've been working on getting those families a place to live. The owners seemed agreeable to letting them stay in the company houses till we could find something else, but now management up and moved their stuff out on the road and locked up the houses. These pitiful women and their children have no place to go. The union's giving the families a little cash, and old Jeb Crumb said we could use his pastureland to put up some tents."

Charles knew of the cave-in. Mining accidents happened all the time around these hills. It was part of the life. "Makes me glad I got out of here when I did."

"How do you like living out West? Seattle, isn't it?" asked Ralph.

"It's pretty wide open. Lots of opportunities. A man can make his own way, that's for sure. Took me a while to get used to the rain, but I don't miss these summers. I reckon Sadie misses her kin, but I've got no regrets. Have you seen the morning paper yet?"

Two young girls came bounding in to Leonetti's giggling about something. Charles watched as they each picked out a donut. The older one reached in her handbag and handed the baker a yellow slip.

"Sorry, gals," said Mr. Leonetti, "but I can't take mine script, just good ole US dollars."

Charles and Ralph watched as the girls turned toward the door, eyes down. Charles slipped twenty cents to the store-keeper who came from behind the counter and handed the girls the donuts before they left the bakery.

"How is Nell?" Ralph asked, as he watched them leave.

"She's out of the woods, but her foot is still a bit sore. It put a hell of a scare in all of us. Nell was damn lucky that Cecelia took on that copperhead. That was one big son of a bitch."

"I'm awful proud of Cecelia. She's tough as nails," said Ralph, pulling out a pack of Camels and offering one to Charles.

"Thanks, don't mind if I do," said Charles, lighting the cigarette.

"I wouldn't argue with that statement," said Charles, as he took a long drag. "Seen the paper? You're a lawyer. What do you think?"

"I'm not surprised. Word on the street is that Sidney Williams most likely dumped the body but that someone else killed her—someone who really wanted her dead. Look at how she died. A lot of rage there," said Ralph. "And, get this. I heard that the judge for the grand jury was Thompson's hunting buddy and the chairman of the jury, Thompson's boss at the bank. No way Thompson was going to get indicted."

"Nothin' changes, does it?" said Charles.

"No. Still dealing with graft and hush money and the Negro getting the shaft. Don't expect it will change any time soon, either. I do know that if the Williams' boy was messing with that Gannon woman like he claims, he's a goner no matter who killed her."

With that he took a last gulp of coffee, snuffed out his cigarette, and pushed back his chair.

"Better get back to work. Tell Kitty I'll swing by tomorrow. I promised Cecelia I'd bring her by for a visit."

Charles drove home with the new fence posts and a bale of chicken wire for the new coop. He planned to set the posts before suppertime.

SIXTEEN

FAITH WAS SITTING ON THE back steps Saturday morning when Ralph pulled up in the alley behind the Cole house with Cecelia as promised. George and Charles were setting the last pole around the old chicken coop.

"Come on in, you two," said George to his brother and niece. "Sadie got up early to make cinnamon rolls, and the coffee is hot."

Cecelia gave Faith a little hug as they headed to the kitchen.

"We can't stay long. Got business up at the Peach Creek Mine this afternoon, but we do want to check on Nell."

Nell was in the parlor playing a spirited game of "Go Fish" with Marion and Rusty. When Cecelia walked in, Nell jumped up and put her arms around her younger cousin.

"Oh, Cecelia. Papa told me how you killed that copperhead. I still can't believe it! You saved my life."

Cecelia hugged her tightly and said, "I mostly did it without thinking. I was just so mad at that snake for biting you. It wasn't till Faith's daddy brought the thing home that I saw how big he was."

Sadie brought a plate of cinnamon rolls into the parlor, followed by Kitty with cups of coffee.

"How are the mine widows doing, Ralph?" asked Kitty.

"We got 'em moved to Crumb's farm; they're living in tents with their children. Better than nothing but it ain't much," said Ralph. "They're getting some handouts, but they need so much more."

"We can help," said Sadie.

"That's great. If you can get something together, Cecelia and I can take it up to the families this afternoon," said Ralph.

"Stay for lunch. We'll have something ready for you to take," said Sadie.

Faith noticed Marion whispering something in Rusty's ear and him nodding.

"Can we go to Peach Creek Drugs and buy penny candy for the kids? We have two bits," said Rusty."

"That's a mighty fine gesture," said Ralph, as he jostled Rusty's hair and gave Marion a kiss on her cheek. "The kids up at the camp haven't had much in the way of treats for a very long time."

Faith helped Aunt Kitty carry boxes of towels, blankets, and used clothes to the car. Charles followed with another box that Sadie had loaded with jars of jam, pickles, a can of coffee, onions and beans from Kitty's garden, and a bag of flour.

"Can Nell and I ride out with you?" said Faith to Nell's Uncle Ralph.

"Cecelia would love the company."

The girls climbed in the back seat.

At Crumb's farm, the tent camp was more desperate than Faith had imagined. The tents were scattered on a pasture with very little shade. Only two outhouses serviced the ten families, and all the cooking was done over open fires. Water had to be carried in buckets from a creek a quarter mile away.

"This is awful, Uncle Ralph. They're out in the hot sun and no tables," said Nell.

Ralph met Nell's eyes and said, "We're working on just that. I've got some union fellows comin' out tomorrow to build some tables and benches and to put up some tarps over the tables for shade. That should help some."

Lugging the boxes of food, clothes, and bedding, the three girls followed Uncle Ralph to a tent near the car.

"This is Mrs. Banchero's place. She's in charge of handing out the donations. We're all doing everything we can, but the union only has so much money," said Ralph.

A haggard woman wearing a food-stained apron peeked out of her tent and waved at Ralph. She squinted and wiped her eyes with her sleeve.

"Morning, Mrs. Banchero. Got some food and other stuff for the families. This is my daughter, Cecelia, and her two cousins Nell and Faith."

Faith held out her hand to the woman. "Nice to meet you."

Mrs. Banchero shook her hand but didn't say anything. Faith noted a vacant stare.

Ralph looked over the field, heat shimmering off it, and said, "I've got some fellows coming over tomorrow to rig up some canvas to give you all a little shade. They're also going to bring some lumber we rounded up and build a couple of tables and benches."

"Our sister and brother sent candy for the children," said Faith, as she reached in one of the boxes and held out the bag of penny candy.

"The children are over yonder playing stickball," said the woman. "Go on over and pass it out."

The three girls walked across the field to where the children were playing. There were so many more children than they had anticipated, but there was enough candy for each child to pick two pieces. Unlike most kids when it came to sweets, these children seemed reluctant to eat the candy. Most tucked it into a pocket or the bib of their overhauls. *That's strange*, thought Faith.

Back in the car the mood was somber. "It was so sad, Papa," said Cecelia. "When we passed out the candy, the kids reached in the bag and took just one piece. They didn't eat it, just put it in their pockets. When we told them they could have two, they couldn't believe it. Still, just a couple of them ate the second one."

"I'll never forget their eyes," said Faith. "They were beyond sad, just lifeless."

SEVENTEEN

THAT SAME AFTERNOON, GEORGE AND Charles went out back to rebuild the chicken coop now that the new posts were up and set. Kitty had been nagging George to fix it for six months, and George was grateful to Charles for taking the project on.

"She actually claimed the chickens weren't laying well because their roosts were rickety. That's the damnedest thing I ever heard, but if gettin' a new coop hushes her up, it's worth it," chuckled George.

Charles laughed as he nailed shingles to the roof, careful not to swallow any of the ones he held between his lips. They had already framed the sides of the henhouse and built fine new roosts inside for Kitty's six laying hens. All that was left was to finish up the shingles and nail new chicken wire to the posts so the birds wouldn't roam the alley any more.

"These gals have a finer house than most of the neighbors," said Charles.

"Heard down at the rail yard Friday that Oscar Grayson was on the grand jury. He's Thompson's boss at the bank," said George, as he took a plug of tobacco from a pouch in his pocket and tucked it in his left cheek.

"Sounds to me like the whole damn jury was rigged from the get-go. Sidney didn't stand a chance."

"That's the way things work in Logan County. You know that," said George, as he stepped back to look at their handiwork.

Charles put up the last three shingles on the henhouse before he replied. "That's true, but it's not this bad everywhere. I don't have to grease anyone's pockets in Seattle. Sadie and I have been running the lunch counter for twelve years, and all I have to do is pay my taxes and keep my business license current and no one bothers us. Goons and cops have been shaking down the businesses in Logan County for years. Those poor suckers are getting it from all sides."

George spit out a mouthful of tobacco juice on the ground. "Let's get that chicken wire up and head to the Peach Pit before the gals find something more for us to fix," said George. "We can down a beer or two before they notice we're gone." He chuckled to himself.

The Pit was full, as was the case most Saturday afternoons. Fellows got paid Friday night and so they had a few nickels jingling in their pockets. Groups of men were either talking about the fight the night before at Madison Square Garden or the latest gossip about the grand jury announcement on Thursday. One man spoke to no one in particular. "I heard that someone's paying for meals to be sent over to the colored's cell from the Smokehouse Restaurant. Only Negro I've ever heard of who's gotten the royal treatment."

George and Charles had just ordered their second beer when a coworker of George's from the rail yard settled on a stool next to them at the bar. "Hey, George, how's it goin'?"

"Hey there, Harvey. Meet my brother-in-law, Charles."

The two men shook hands, Harvey ordered a beer and began to tell them about an encounter he'd had in Logan early that morning. "I was having coffee and donuts at Leonetti's this morning when Bart Strout came in. He's the reporter who's been covering the Gannon murder. Told me the sheriff's office is going to offer a $10,000 reward for information that leads to a conviction in Mrs. Gannon's murder."

"Whoa, I thought they just indicted the colored fellow for her murder. This thing is getting crazier by the minute," said Charles. "If they've got the guy, why the reward? Makes no sense."

George downed his beer and set the glass on the bar. "It's clear as mud that no one thinks Sidney's the murderer. I bet the Klan got to him and threatened his family. It's the only thing that makes sense."

Charles put his glass down and shook his head. "Poor bugger. I don't think we'll ever find out who did it. Too many suspects. Think we'll ever learn who was on Gloria's list of sixteen?"

Harvey ordered a second beer and said, "Not a chance in hell."

EIGHTEEN

FAITH WAS EXCITED AS NELL brushed her hair. Uncle George was taking the two families to dinner after church at Bertha's Diner. Bertha was acclaimed for her fried chicken dinner with sky-high buttermilk biscuits.

"I think you ladies deserve a day off from the kitchen. What do you think, Sadie?" George had asked.

"It seems like a big extravagance to me, but it's a fine gesture on your part," said Sadie.

"Leave it to mama to turn any positive into a negative." said Faith to Nell. "Why couldn't she just say thank you?"

Nell brushed Faith's hair a little harder.

"Ouch," said Faith.

"Oh, hush. I read in *Good Housekeeping* that you should brush your hair one hundred strokes a day to make it shine. Sometimes I think you are a little hard on Aunt Sadie. She has raised you and Marion way out in Seattle with no family around, and then there's the whole thing of losing your little sister, Rebecca."

"Maybe you're right, but I'm just tired of Mother always being a wet blanket."

It was the first time the families had had a meal at a restaurant together, and the preacher's sermon went on and on.

"Sit still," said Faith, annoyed at Rusty and Marion. They fiddled and fussed all through the sermon, which was aptly based on the parable of the Good Samaritan.

"'And who is my neighbor?' Jesus replied, 'A certain man was going down from Jerusalem to Jericho, and he fell among robbers, and they stripped him and beat him and went off leaving him half dead. And by chance a certain priest was going down the road, and when he saw him, he passed on the other side. And, likewise a Levite, also, when he came to the place and saw him, passed on the other side.

"But a certain Samaritan, who was on a journey, saw him and took compassion on him, and came to him and bandaged his wounds, pouring oil and wine on them, and he put him on his own beast and brought him to an inn and took care of him.'"

Reverend Corn continued, "Let this lesson dwell in your own hearts, dear friends, and live the message. There are so many in our own community who can use our help in these desperate times. Open your hearts and your pockets."

"How much longer, Faith," said Marion, tugging on her sister's sleeve. "We got enough religion for the week."

"Shush, Marion."

Faith searched the pews for Henry, but he wasn't anywhere to be found. "Henry didn't come. I don't blame him," Faith whispered to Nell. Her mother's reprimand from last Sunday still smarted.

Faith loved the choir at First Baptist. This morning, dressed in white robes with burgundy trim, they sang a beautiful rendition of "Nearer, My God, to Thee," one of Faith's favorites. Mrs. Melton accompanied the choir on the old pipe organ, and Faith thought, uncharitably, that she could have done a better job. *Maybe I should offer my services to Reverend Corn again*, she thought.

Faith played the organ at the Emanuel Baptist Church the family attended a few blocks off Broadway. It was a new congregation in a brand new church and the preacher was thrilled when Faith volunteered to play for the choir. She had never had formal piano lessons but had a good ear, knew her chords, and could pick up any tune. It took her a couple of weeks to master the pipes but once she had them figured out, she was as good as any of the organists she had heard at the big First Baptist downtown. *I'd add a longer introduction if I were playing*, she thought.

It was after noon when Reverend Corn finally sprung them loose, as Rusty put it. Faith could smell the salty fried chicken a block from the restaurant. The Coles and Dansworths sat at a large oak table in the middle of Bertha's Diner. Charles was already there. He gave all the girls a peck on the cheek and jostled Rusty's flame-red hair. The talk was lively around the table. Kitty bragged on the men and the fine job that they did on the henhouse.

"It's the finest coop in all of Peach Creek, and I swear those hens are laying more eggs already," said Kitty.

Bellows of laughter came from deep in George's gut as he took a bite of buttermilk biscuit dripping with butter and honey. "Glad to oblige you, Mrs. Cole. Anything to make you happy." He leaned over and gave her a peck on the cheek, and Faith noticed the twinkle in his eye.

The restaurant was full of Sunday diners and folks turned their heads to their table at all the merriment. The chicken lived up to its reputation, Rusty taking the last leg on the platter.

"I swear that boy is growing like Kitty's Kentucky Wonder beans," laughed Charles. "I bet none of his long pants fit him when school starts up in September."

Rusty grinned as he continued to clean the bone.

They were all deciding on whether to have berry or lemon meringue pie for dessert when Faith felt a breeze from the front door swinging open. Robert and Hazel Thompson and Henry walked in. Everyone in the restaurant turned and stared. The place went silent like the woods after a winter snowfall. Faith sat frozen in her seat.

"Have you got a table for us, Bertha?" asked Mr. Thompson.

Bertha seated the family at a small table in the back by the kitchen door. Faith saw the diners watch their every move as the merry spirit of the dining room dissipated. People who had been lingering actually asked for their checks and pushed back their chairs to leave. The Thompsons were being shunned as surely as if they were a family of witches from Salem, Massachusetts.

"Quit staring, Marion. It's rude," said Faith.

Papa tried to change the conversation to Elizabeth's big shindig that was coming up the following Saturday night.

"So, are you and Nell going to help Aunt Elizabeth and Cecelia get ready for Kitty's birthday party?" he asked Faith.

Faith was paying no attention to her father but thinking instead of the humiliation Henry must be feeling, sitting there in silence with his mother and father. What she didn't know was that this was a celebration supper of sorts for the Thompson family because of Henry's father's release from jail. It was the first time Hazel Thompson had left her house since her husband's arrest, and she was only here for Henry's sake.

"Faith, did you hear me?" asked Papa.

Faith looked at him vacantly, then glanced in Nell's direction. Nell was almost glaring at her and slightly shaking her head. Nonetheless, Faith pushed back her chair and walked over to the Thompsons' table. She held out her hand to Henry's mother who looked pale and worn out. "Hello, Mrs. Thompson. I'm Faith Dansworth from Seattle, Washington, and I'm a friend of Henry's. Hi, Henry, it's good to see you."

"Please sit down," said Hazel Thompson in a surprisingly gravelly voice.

"Oh, thank you, but I'm with my family, and we are just finishing up. I just wanted to say hello. It's great to see you out with your family."

Henry barely lifted his eyes from the menu when she spoke. He said nothing.

Faith could feel all eyes in the restaurant were on her as she turned and walked back to her table. She held her back straight and her head high. Faith could feel that her ears remained a perfectly normal soft pink.

No one at the table said anything, but Nell gave her one of her now-familiar eye rolls.

"What? I was only using good manners," said Faith in her cousin's direction.

Rusty broke the ice. "If you don't want your berry pie, Faith, I'll eat it."

"Dream on, little cousin," Faith replied with a chuckle as she took a bite.

NINETEEN

EXCITEMENT WAS HIGH AS IT was only a week until Aunt Kitty's fortieth birthday party at Elizabeth's in Logan. Nell and Cecelia came to Faith's aid with her yellow party dress. The tulle was so delicate that Faith had difficulty keeping the stitches straight. The seams kept bunching up under the needle on the treadle sewing machine.

"Damn it!" said Faith as another seam gathered and the machine stalled.

"I didn't realize how impatient you could be," said Nell, pushing Faith away from the machine and taking over on the stitching.

In addition, there was so much handwork that Faith would never have finished it in time for the party without Nell and Cecelia's help. Faith was good with crocheting so she worked on the lace sleeve trim. Cecelia made tiny pleats on the bodice using an almost invisible stitch. "Precious taught me," said Cecelia, a little wistfully.

Besides helping Faith with her complicated dress, the girls also were assigned to get Rusty's room ready for Aunt Alma from Ohio. They stripped the sheets from Rusty's bed and dusted and mopped his room.

"Why do I always have to give up my room?" asked Rusty, as Faith filled his arms with a load of sheets to take to the back porch.

"Because you're the baby," Nell retorted.

Faith was on a mission to have the room shine for her aunt. She planned to fill it with Aunt Kitty's yellow roses on the day Aunt Alma arrived. Mama and Papa were picking Alma up at the Front on Friday morning.

On Thursday afternoon Charles drove Faith and Nell into Logan. Nell had an appointment with Doc Howard, a follow-up to the snakebite that seemed eons ago.

Nell and Faith planned to go to the five-and-dime to buy decorations for the party and then get flapper Cokes before Nell's appointment. They were walking past the *Logan Tribune* offices on Stratton. Nell noticed a stack of today's papers piled up for sale outside their door. The headline blared, "County Offers $10,000 Reward Leading to Conviction in Gannon Murder."

"Let's buy one," said Nell.

Faith found a nickel in her purse and dropped it in the box before she picked up a copy from the pile. When they got to the dime store, both girls ordered their Cokes and settled on stools. Faith opened the paper and smoothed it out on the countertop. "You read it out loud, Faith."

Faith read to Nell about the reward.

"Go on, Faith," said Nell.

"In a letter written to his sister, Sidney Williams states: 'Someday they'll catch the killer. I think he's long gone. All I know is that neither Mr. Thompson or me is guilty.' Mr. Williams' supper is being delivered to him from the Smokehouse Restaurant."

"Doesn't that seem odd to you, Nell?"

"Well, I never heard of a colored, especially one who's supposed to have had relations with a white woman and then killed her, being treated so special. It's more likely that the Klan would have strung him up by now."

Faith shivered.

"So why the heck did they let Henry's dad go and not Sidney?" asked Faith. "He's got as much blood on his hands as Sidney, don't you think?"

"This is West Virginia. I've lived my whole life here and believe me, nothing ever, ever changes. It's never going to, either. Can't you see that by now?"

"No I can't," said Faith. "I believe in justice. I know it will prevail no matter what you say."

What could Sidney's motive be for killing Gloria? thought Faith It was such a violent death and the Sidney she had met, the one who tenderly brought Marion back to them with Broadway in her pocket, didn't seem to have a mean bone in his body.

The blue shoe came to mind, and Faith still didn't know what Henry was going to do with it. And where was the other shoe? She hadn't told anyone about the find, not even Nell.

"None of it makes sense. It just had to be one of those men on the list, don't you think?" I'm positive that there's no way Sidney will be convicted of the murder," said Faith. Nell did her now-familiar eye roll, but she didn't say anything.

They finished their Cokes and agreed to meet in front of the courthouse where Charles was scheduled to pick them up in an hour. Nell took off one way to Doc Howard's and Faith the opposite to window shop at McDonald's Department Store. She had just turned the corner when she saw Henry coming out of the bank. He looked at her and turned in the opposite direction.

"Henry, wait up."

Faith hurried to catch up with him. Henry didn't slow down and kept his eyes on the sidewalk. Faith had trouble keeping up on her short legs. "Hey, is something the matter?"

Henry turned around and glared at Faith.

"I don't want your help," Henry said in a louder than usual voice. "You've already embarrassed me more than once. Please don't do it again."

Faith was stunned and sucked in her breath. He might as well have punched her in the stomach. "What are you talking about?"

"At church. I don't want you defending me. And then again at Bertha's. Just leave me alone."

Faith felt her face flush with a rush of blood. Her heart was beating wildly, and it crossed her mind that Henry could see it pounding in her chest.

"Don't worry. It won't happen ever again."

She spit out the words and then couldn't think of anything else to say, so she turned around and started to walk back the other way.

Henry tried to backtrack. "Wait, Faith, I didn't mean it like that. Let me . . ."

She was now running down the sidewalk, red curls flying, tears welling up.

Faith tried not to show how upset she was when she met Nell for their ride. She hardly said a word on the short trip back to Peach Creek for fear she'd burst out in tears. Once inside, she hurried up to the bedroom and flung herself across the bed on her stomach. Faith couldn't hold back any longer. Rivulets of tears flowed down her cheeks and onto the pillowcase, staining it pink from the rouge Faith has applied so carefully that morning.

"It's Henry, isn't it? Did you see him while I was at Doc Howard's? What did he say, Faith? Please tell me," pleaded Nell.

"I wish I could die, I just wish I could die," was all Faith could muster. "How could he, how could he?" The sobs got louder as she gulped in air and sucked big globs of snot back up her nose. "Go down and get your Mama's kitchen knife. I just want to plunge it through my heart. That's the only thing that will make this pain go away."

Nell was helpless. Faith rejected every attempt Nell made at consoling her. Like the good friend that she was, Nell simply waited it out. The sobs faded to whimpers, and the tears dried until there was nothing left but Faith crumpled, hair matted, eyes swollen, red cheeks stained and blotchy, and nose still running.

"I'm going to make you a cup of chamomile tea and then come back up and we will talk," said Nell. She threw Faith a handkerchief that must have belonged to her pa, the kind you need when you have a raging cold and the dainty embroidered ones just won't do. "And I'm not bringing Mama's knife, so don't you be gettin' any more crazy ideas!" said Nell, as she headed down the stairs to put the kettle on.

Finally, Faith gathered herself up and sipped the hot tea.

"It was awful, Nell. His eyes were so cold. He said that he didn't want me defending him ever again."

"For goodness sake, Faith. Men don't like their women-folk taking charge. It's supposed to be the other way around. Surely you know that."

Faith reached for the handkerchief and blew her nose so hard it sounded like the C&O was coming through their bedroom. "He's lucky to have me by his side—no one else is. But if he wants to stand alone and have all of Logan County humiliate him, then let him. Serves him right."

"Maybe he just found out some terrible news or something and you caught him off guard," said Nell. "The grand jury only finished up last week and it's all over town now about the things his daddy's done with Mrs. Gannon. It said they'd been carrying on for two years and all those "fox hunts" were nothin' more than rendezvous for you know what. Think how you'd feel if it was your daddy was doin' those things and then Bart Strout displays all your family's dirty laundry on the front page of the *Tribune*. Talk about humiliation. The one I feel sorry for is Henry's mom."

Nell was now curled up in the old wingback chair with her long legs draped over one of the arms. The upholstery was frayed and threadbare, so Nell had covered it in one of her granny's quilts. It was the coziest spot in the house. "You're in love with him, aren't you?" she asked.

"No, I hate him," said Faith.

"Well, I think it's time you spill the beans and tell me what really happened on the Fourth when the two of you disappeared for over an hour," said Nell. "And the whole truth, Missy. Don't leave anything out."

Without much more coaxing, Faith described her trip to Trace Mountain with Henry. She described her fall, the kiss, but she gave no mention of the muddy blue shoe with the brass button that was now stowed away in her grip just feet away. It seemed like a betrayal if she told Nell about the shoe. But it did feel good to release the secret feelings she had bottled up for two weeks inside her. "I know it was a sin to let him kiss me like that, Nell, but I couldn't stop it."

"Heck, if Henry Thompson was kissin' me, I wouldn't want him to stop either. I'm jealous."

Nell got up and lay on the bed next to Faith. She covered them both with a World War I army blanket.

"I just don't understand men. How could he be so mean?" said Faith.

"I know you don't believe it now, Faith, but Henry still loves you. You must forgive him. Just keep your distance for now, and give him a little space. Even if he doesn't believe it, he needs you now more than ever."

There was a long silence, and then Nell began to talk again. She finally came up for air, but Faith hadn't heard a thing. She was fast asleep, her matted red curls stuck to the pillow.

TWENTY

AUNT ALMA BLEW IN WITH the morning train, smelling of violets and talcum powder. Marion put on her beloved hat and insisted on riding with Charles and Sadie to pick Alma up. Faith went out to the garden in the early morning to pick an armload of yellow roses. She arranged them in Aunt Kitty's large cut-glass vase from Fenton Glass, a hundred miles north of Peach Creek. It had been a wedding present, and Kitty held it dear. Faith placed the roses on the dresser in Rusty's room. Their scent filled the little room. Opening the windows and fluffing the pillows on the newly made bed, Faith thought, *I just want everything perfect for Aunt Alma.* Faith was looking out the upstairs window when Charles drove up. Marion hopped out and yelled through the screen door, "She's here!"

Faith bounded down the stairs and was greeted with an enormous hug.

"I'll get your grip," said Rusty. "You're sleeping in my room."

"Why, thank you. Don't believe I've seen you since you were a baby. You've grown into a fine young man."

Rusty blushed and ran up the stairs.

Alma turned to Nell. "I hear you girls have made dresses that are the cat's meow for Kitty's party. You must model them for me. Sadie wrote and told me the colors, so I got you a little something to wear with them."

Marion let out a sigh. Alma saw that sad-eyed look of hers and said, "I got something special just for you, too, Marion."

Marion's face lit up, and she squeezed Alma so hard around the middle that Alma almost fell over backward.

"Girls, girls. Let Alma get off the porch and sit down. She's had a long train ride," said Kitty. "I've got a pot of coffee on and a rhubarb pie waiting. Come on in. We're all so glad you came."

When everyone was settled around the kitchen table, Alma said, "So tell me all about tomorrow's shindig."

Before anyone else could get a word in, Nell began, "It's at seven tomorrow and everyone and their cousin's uncle has been invited. Faith and I are going early to help decorate. Aunt Elizabeth said that we're going to roll up the rugs and push the furniture back so there's room for dancing. And we're making punch and birthday cake and her colored maid is fixing her famous chicken-salad finger sandwiches and . . ."

"You're giving it all away, Nell. There'll be no surprises left for Aunt Kitty," interrupted Faith.

"Well, I can't wait. I brought my dancing shoes," said Alma.

Alma left the table and went upstairs. "I'll be right back," she said. She came down with five packages. She gave one to each of the three girls. There were lovely beaded evening bags in colors to match Nell and Faith's dresses and an elaborate hair clip decorated with rhinestones and ribbons for Marion. Marion was, of course, dazzled by all the sparkle. She took off her hat and asked Alma to put the clip in her hair. She rushed to the mirror over the buffet in the dining room to admire herself.

"Who's that one for?" asked Rusty, as he eyed a package wrapped in violet paper and ribbon.

Aunt Alma replied, "That's for your cousin, Cecelia. I haven't met her but I got the impression she's quite refined. It's a beaded purse like Nell's except in black and silver."

There was no hiding the disappointment in Rusty's eyes.

"I didn't forget you," Alma said, handing the last package to Rusty.

He unwrapped it and found a cap gun with a fake leather holster that he quickly secured around his waist. With a grin spread clear across his face, Rusty bolted out the back door to try it out.

"Hey there, young man. What do you say to Aunt Alma?"

A loud "thank you" rang out through the back yard along with cap gun shots.

"Stay clear of my hens, young man," said Kitty. "I want them to keep on layin'."

"Alma, you spoil the children," said Sadie.

TWENTY-ONE

THE NEXT AFTERNOON AS FAITH carefully laid her dress over the back seat and climbed in, she let out a sigh.

"Why the sad face, Sweet Pea?" asked Charles, looking at her in the rearview mirror. "This is the big day you've been waiting for."

Papa was right. The sun was shining, and a sweet little breeze blew off the creek.

"Nothing. I'm fine," said Faith.

It wasn't true. She had hardly slept last night fretting over whether Henry would show up at the party, and if he did, would they even speak. Faith had dreamt about tonight and imagined dancing in Henry's arms in her yellow voile dress. Now her plans were dashed. Nell turned around and gave her cousin a knowing look.

There was no time for moping once they got to Aunt Elizabeth's. "I told Bessie to save the cake decorating for you girls. She made Kitty's favorite hummingbird cake. Kitty says Bessie's cake is so good it makes people hum." Elizabeth laughed at her own joke. "We made three cakes, we're expecting so many friends, so you better get hopping."

Faith still was starry eyed by the opulence of the house and today even more so. The chandelier sparkled and the silver, polished and waiting for nuts and candies and tea sandwiches, caught the light from the chandelier and was reflected in the gilt mirror that hung above the sideboard. The three girls set out pink candles on every available flat surface they could find.

In the kitchen Faith noticed a change in Nell when it came to her cousin, Cecelia. All the jealousy seemed to have melted away. When Cecelia dropped a big glob of green frosting where the "i" in "Elizabeth" needed to be dotted, Nell dipped her finger in and removed it and then popped it in her mouth in one quick movement.

"That's OK, Cecelia. Gave me an excuse to taste the buttercream."

All three girls laughed. Cecelia looked at Faith, and Faith could sense the relief in her eyes.

After the cakes were frosted, Nell, Faith, and Cecelia started on the pink and green streamers, Kitty's favorite colors. They hung them in swags from every light fixture and banister. They rolled up the Persian rug in the parlor, and Aunt Elizabeth helped them push all the furniture against the walls. Then she sprinkled cornmeal all over the inlaid hardwood floor. "Now we can really cut a rug," said Elizabeth. "I'm looking forward to watching you gals out there tonight." Faith felt a lump in her throat and a rock in her stomach.

Guests began arriving at seven sharp. Faith knew she looked pretty, maybe not beautiful like her cousin Nell with her shiny dark hair, long legs, and ivory skin, and not fashionable like Cecelia in a store-bought lavender silk dress—from a fancy Charleston department store—that barely covered her knees. Faith was cute with her unruly red curls caught up in a yellow satin ribbon that matched her dress perfectly. The yellow voile skimmed her body just enough to show off her curves, landing above her narrow ankles.

"You were right, Nell. Yellow is a good color on me," said Faith.

"Wait till Henry sees you," said Nell. "He'll keel over."

"I don't care if he drops dead," said Faith. Deep down, she hoped that she would break his heart like he broke hers. "I plan to dance with every boy here. To heck with Henry—if he even bothers to show up."

It was the fanciest party that Faith had ever attended. The rooms glowed in the candlelight and the sparkle of the crystal and silver. The table and sideboard in the dining room held platters of fancy sandwiches and the three hummingbird cakes. Bob Barley and the Banjo Boys filled the house with lively music and a few brave souls were already dancing to the tunes in the parlor. Faith laughed to herself as she watched Aunt Alma out on the dance floor with Cecelia's father, Ralph.

Aunt Alma wasn't kidding when she said she brought her dancing shoes, thought Faith.

As Faith stood in the hall greeting guests, she felt so conflicted, hoping to see Henry and dreading seeing him at the same time. The house was packed with old friends and family, and happy sounds emerged from all the rooms, but there was no sign of Henry. It was close to nine when Aunt Elizabeth directed the band to stop the music. She tapped a spoon on her glass hoping to get everyone's attention. When that didn't work, Nell put both index fingers in her mouth and gave an ear-piercing whistle that made everyone stop in their tracks.

"You've got to teach me how to do that," laughed Cecelia.

"Thank you all for coming to help us celebrate Kitty's fortieth birthday. We're about to cut the cake, so come squeeze into the dining room," Elizabeth announced.

Faith was about to join everyone when Marion opened the front door, and Henry walked in. She refused to acknowledge him. Not looking in his direction, she moved to the dining room and began singing "Happy Birthday" with the crowd. Aunt Kitty was blowing out her candles, all forty of them, when Faith felt two hands on her shoulders from behind. She shivered and felt that now-familiar warmth deep inside her.

"You look beautiful," Henry whispered in her ear.

She pulled away and went to wish Aunt Kitty a happy birthday without even turning around. Faith picked up a wrapped package and handed it to her aunt.

"It's for you," she said. Then without waiting for Aunt Kitty to open the gift she had taken a month to crochet—the green shawl—she walked very deliberately through the kitchen and out onto the back porch. She needed some air and a minute to compose herself. Faith's eyes welled up and she clenched her fists.

I will not let him make me cry, so help me, she said to herself.

While the evening breeze cooled her down (both literally and figuratively), she heard a car door slam and some gruff male voices in the distance. But she saw no car lights.

I wonder who that could be, she thought.

Then the screen door opened with a creak, and Henry stood there looking at her.

"I meant it, you really do look beautiful. Won't you come and dance with me?" said Henry.

"I don't want to dance with you, Henry Thompson."

Faith turned on her heel, red curls swinging. Brushing past Henry, Faith walked back into the party. She could feel Henry's eyes on her, watching her retreat. Both Cecelia and Nell had found dance partners and had joined Aunt Alma on the crowded dance floor. Without any hesitation, Faith marched right up to Walter Schmitz, knowing he was one of Henry's football buddies, and asked him to dance with her. He was surprised but pleased.

"Why, thank you, I'd be honored."

Walter gave her a little old-fashioned bow and took her hand, steering her through the dancers. The Banjo Boys were playing a fox-trot. Faith was surprised how light on his feet Walter was given his bulk. He led her firmly, one hand on her waist, through the lively steps of the dance. Faith saw Henry watching her from the hall.

I hope your black heart is ripping to shreds, she thought.

Walter was just about to send her into a dip when Henry stepped up and tapped Walter's shoulder.

"May I cut?"

Faith shook her head at Walter.

"I don't think the lady wants to dance with you," said Walter.

Henry's face turned red. Faith had humiliated him, and she instantly regretted her actions. Henry pulled his arm back, his hand in a fist ready to punch Walter. Before the punch landed, Faith heard a loud crack and saw a flash of white light behind her eyes that sent her to the floor in a puddle of yellow voile. When Faith woke up, she was on one of the green horsehair sofas still pushed up against the walls in Elizabeth's parlor.

"What happened? Did Henry hit me?"

She reached up and touched her head above her left eyebrow. It was sticky and wet. Faith was bleeding. Doc Howard was leaning over her.

"Goodness no," said the doctor. You were hit by a brick and you were knocked out. I'm afraid you may have to have stitches. We need to get you to my office."

Around her, the partygoers were hushed. Bob Barley and the Banjo Boys stood with banjos and fiddles lifeless at their sides, and her family hovered over her, worried looks on their faces. Marion was holding her hand. Faith was confused and sleepy. She had a throbbing headache. She struggled to keep her eyes open. She did see Henry, Walter, and Nell, worried looks on their faces, standing behind the doctor. He was shaking her gently.

"Stay with us, Faith. Don't fall asleep," said Dr. Howard.

Cecelia found a blanket and gave it to Sadie who wrapped it around Faith. Charles and George lifted Faith up, carried her gently to the back door, and put her in the back seat of Ralph's car.

"I'll get the bastards who did this, Charles," said Ralph, as he got behind the wheel. "This was directed squarely at me. They're not gonna get away with this. This time they've gone too damn far."

Charles sat next to Ralph in the front seat. Sadie got in next to Faith and held her daughter's bleeding head in her lap as Ralph drove them to Dr. Howard's office on Front Street.

Inside the Banjos Boys began another tune as soon as the glass was swept up.

"Let's not let this spoil Kitty's birthday," said Elizabeth to her guests, although she was badly shaken. The party was clearly over.

Several men, including Henry and Walter, led by Elizabeth's husband Morris, searched the perimeter of the house, but there was no sign of the perpetrators. They had driven away before the bricks hit the window.

PART THREE

AUGUST 1932
THE TRIAL

THE PEACHES HUNG SO THICK and heavy on the trees lining the main street of Peach Creek that the neighbors put poles and crutches under the overburdened limbs to support them. What used to be hard green balls were now lush, round peaches, blushing soft pinks and oranges. They only needed a week more in the hot August sun until they would ripen to glorious, juicy perfection.

TWENTY-TWO

"Won't be long before we're treated to the smell of peach pie baking in the oven," said Charles. He and Sadie had Sunday supper cleanup. Sadie washed and Charles dried.

"I'm looking forward to sinking my teeth into a peach right off the tree," said Sadie. "The peaches we get in Seattle don't hold a candle to these here in Peach Creek. There's just never enough heat to sweeten them up. Sometimes I actually dream about Peach Creek peaches!" she said, putting the last plate back in the cupboard. "We sure had some wonderful summers when Kitty and I were girls—not a care in the world. Our biggest concern was when the peaches would ripen. Things just seemed so much simpler."

"Lots has happened since then, Sadie. Too much heartache, that's for sure, but some good things too." Charles hung the damp towel on the handle of the woodstove to dry. "All you have to do is look at our children. We should be right proud."

The air in the kitchen stood still. Sadie stiffened with her hands on the sink. She could hear the rest of the family squabbling and laughing over a move on the Parcheesi board, the happy clatter of a family comfortable with each other, as natural as if they had all grown up in the same house, not just living together for two months.

Charles knew what Sadie couldn't say out loud and just decided to say it for her. Everyone had been dancing around the topic all summer and he believed it was time to get it all out once and for all.

"Forgive me if I'm out of line, but I'm just going to say this. I know this trip has been difficult for you, but I think it's time that you faced that baby's death. I need you, Faith needs you, and Marion needs you. Until you confront this full force you simply can't give your best to us. Your heart has been aching for too damn long. It wasn't your fault. No one blames you, but it's high time you forgive yourself and get on with living."

Sadie had her back to her husband. Her body began to shake, yet she didn't say anything. She had no words for Charles. Everything he said was true.

She has to stop thinking about the what ifs, thought Charles.

Maybe she could have found a doctor on the train, or maybe she should have gotten off in Cleveland and found a hospital. Maybe she should have left Becky at home with Charles and Faith. None of it mattered.

Now that the topic was out, Charles didn't stop. He had been patient for so very long, maybe too long. "You were grieving for your Mama, Sadie. It was a long, hard trip. Becky had a cold when you started out. And how were you to know that the chicken pox would fly through that train like wildfire? And then there was the lonely train ride home to Seattle all by yourself. It must have been horrible. There's no denying it was a terrible tragedy, but it was no one's fault, no one's."

He walked to the sink and took Sadie in his arms.

"I'm so sorry I didn't grab Faith and get us on a train to Peach Creek to take care of you. I shouldn't have left you there to cope all by yourself," said Charles.

Sadie crumbled like a dry leaf. Just then Faith came through the kitchen door to refill her glass with sweet tea. She looked at her mother weeping in Papa's big embrace. She put her glass down on the damp counter and simply patted her mother's back and finally whispered, "It's OK, Mama, it's OK."

It took a long time to release eleven years of tears, but Charles was a patient man. When Sadie had cried the last tear, Charles wiped her eyes dry, and they went to their room. Charles turned back the bed covers, pulled off Sadie's shoes and stockings and the apron still wrapped around her waist. She let him do all of this as if she were his child. He laid her gently on the bed and climbed in next to her. Sadie curled up beside him and put her head on his shoulder. He smoothed her hair and kissed her eyelids. Her breathing settled down and he could hear a regular rhythm to it.

It won't be long before she's asleep, he thought.

To his surprise, Sadie said, "Charles, I want to go to the cemetery tomorrow. I want to visit Becky's grave—and leave her some flowers—and Mama's grave, too."

"I'll come with you," he said. "We can bring some of Kitty's roses. They'd like that."

Charles and Sadie fell into such a deep and satisfying sleep that they didn't hear Marion as she came in and slipped into her bed.

TWENTY-THREE

CHARLES AND SADIE WERE UP with the birds, even before George, who was usually the one to make the coffee before he headed off to the rail yard for work. Today Charles made the coffee and Sadie had corn bread in the oven and a pot of oatmeal on the back burner long before the rest of the family was padding around the kitchen. A Mason jar heaping over with yellow and pink roses still wet with morning dew sat on the kitchen table.

"Something smells awful damn good," said George, as he poured himself a cup of coffee. He winked at Charles and gave Sadie a little sideways hug as she cut him a square of hot corn bread.

"We're off to the cemetery to pay a visit to Becky and my mama this morning," said Sadie.

Sadie packed George's lunch pail, wrapping his cheese sandwich in waxed paper, filling his thermos with coffee sweetened with three spoonsful of sugar just the way George liked, tucking in an extra molasses cookie.

"I'm grateful that Kitty and the children are still upstairs sleeping in. I don't want to talk about last night or our trip to the cemetery. There'll be plenty of time to share memories with everyone later," said Sadie. "Right now I just want to have you to myself. I need you, Charles Dansworth."

She hugged Charles, left a note on the counter for Kitty that she and Charles would return before lunch.

It was another sultry day and the McConnell Cemetery had almost no trees to provide shade. It had been eleven years since the burials, and it took Sadie and Charles several minutes to find the plots. Becky's and Mama's graves were side by side but the grave markers were almost completely covered with grass. Charles took out his pocketknife, knelt down, and began to cut away the sod from each grave. Then he took out his handkerchief and swiped away the dirt and dust. Sadie got on her knees, too, and touched the first stone. She traced the tiny angel engraved at the top, then the words below:

Rebecca Sarah Dansworth, 1921–1923

Charles put his arm around his wife and Sadie laid her head on his shoulder and let the tears flow freely. Charles wept, too. These were tears that were long in coming, cleansing tears. Sadie placed the roses between the two graves before she spoke.

"Let's say a prayer," she began, standing up. "Our Father which art in heaven, hallowed be Thy name . . ."

Charles's strong voice blended with hers as they stood holding hands. Finally Sadie squeezed her husband's hand.

"Good-bye, Mama. Good-bye, my sweet baby."

Walking back to the truck, Sadie felt visibly lighter.

"Let's stop in town for coffee," said Charles.

Outside Leonetti's, Charles bought a copy of the *Tribune*, ink still damp from the press, and tucked it under his arm, intending to take it home to read when he finished cleaning the basement. It was a chore he had promised Kitty he'd do. She wanted the shelves cleared and dusted, Mason jars carted up to the kitchen, and the packed dirt floor swept before her canning got into full swing. She and Sadie had been calculating the last couple of days how many jars and lids they would need for all the crab apples and peaches they were planning on putting up. They had warned Faith and Nell that they were expected to be there to help. The sisters had even roped Rusty and Marion into the process.

But for now, Sadie and Charles stole a few minutes to themselves over coffee and donuts. "I'm so sorry, Charles. I haven't been much of a . . ."

"It's OK, it's OK," Charles interrupted, putting his hand over hers as it lay on the table. "I feel guilty that I didn't come with you. Maybe Becky'd still be with us if I'd been on the train with the two of you." Charles never moved his hand. "I'm so grateful you came back to me. It must have been so hard."

Sadie looked at her husband and said, "No more 'what ifs.' We are, once and for all, done with that."

TWENTY-FOUR

CECELIA AND UNCLE RALPH CAME out every evening to check on Faith and give the families an update on the mine situation.

"Seems there's no way to prove it was guards from the mine that hit Faith with the brick," Ralph told everyone. "But I did file a writ with the courts complaining of the hostility and treatment of the mine widows and their families following the mine collapse. Don't think it'll make a horse's ass bit of difference though. What is making a difference is that Elizabeth has organized the Women's League to bring meals to the families living out there on Crumb's farm. That sister of ours," he said, looking at George, "is a one-woman force."

Nell and Faith were stretched out on the bed, taking the imposed afternoon rest that Doc Howard demanded after Faith's head injury. They moved over to make room for Cecelia. Faith couldn't help scratching the spot above her left eyebrow with the six stitches, even though Doc Howard had warned her not to. It was exactly a week since Aunt Kitty's party. "I can't wait till Monday when I get my stitches out," said Faith. "They're driving me crazy."

"I can't believe Henry hasn't come to check on you," said Nell. "But you really shouldn't have been so mean to him,

Faith. I mean I know you were hoppin' mad at him, and I don't blame you, but he is so dreamy and I just know in my heart he really loves—"

Faith heard a knock at the front door.

"Maybe it's Henry," said Nell, as she bounced off the bed, taking the stairs two at a time to answer the door.

Faith felt a combination of disappointment and relief that she hadn't heard a word from Henry since she was hit with the brick at Aunt Kitty's birthday party.

How can he stay away? she thought. And yet she knew it was her fault too. Nell was right. She had been pretty mean. Downstairs Faith heard a male voice, but it wasn't familiar, then the screen door banged shut.

"Who was it?" shouted Faith.

Nell climbed the stairs holding the most beautiful bouquet of flowers—an arrangement of yellow roses, white daisies, and ferns in a lovely cut-glass vase from Jackson's Flower Boutique in Logan.

"Look what you got!" said Nell, putting the delicate arrangement on the dresser. "Quick, read the card. Can you believe it? I've never gotten flowers from a real florist or anyone for that matter. I bet it's from Henry."

"I doubt it," said Faith. "Maybe it's from your Aunt Elizabeth or your dad."

"I don't think so," said Cecelia.

Faith wanted it to be from Henry but was afraid to read the card in case it wasn't from him.

"You read it," she said to Cecelia.

Cecelia pulled the card from the flowers where the tiny envelope was tucked in amongst the ferns. It was addressed to "Faith Dansworth."

"OK, here it is," said Cecelia, pulling the note from its tiny envelope. She paused for dramatic effect before reading. "'Hope you are feeling better. I chose flowers to match your dress. Henry.'"

Faith got up and took the note and reread it to herself, not quite believing Cecelia.

"It's in his hand. I recognize his handwriting," said Nell. "Isn't it just too dreamy?"

Faith agreed with her cousin but couldn't quite permit herself to say it out loud just yet. But this really was something. Like Nell, she had never received flowers from a boy, or anyone else, for that matter.

It was late Monday afternoon when Charles suggested that after Faith's appointment he take the kids for a dip in the community pool on the outskirts of Logan. The heat baked down all day making the sidewalks shimmer. Faith passed muster with Doc Howard who took out her stitches and told she her she was out of danger from a concussion and could do most anything she wanted. Right now that anything was cooling off in the pool.

The whole pickup full of kids rushed to the ticket booth. Charles paid the twenty-five cents for each of them and they took turns twirling through the turnstile. Faith couldn't help but notice a line of Negro children lined up shoulder to shoulder on the wrong side of the chain-link fence that surrounded the city pool.

"Nell, don't they have any money to get in? I've got a dollar. Let's go back and get some of those kids. It's so bloody hot they must be melting."

"Are you kidding?" said Nell. "Negroes don't swim in the city pool. Besides most of them don't even know how to swim. Come on, race you to the pool." Faith was so dumbstruck she couldn't think of a reply.

Once on the pool deck, it was clear that they weren't the only ones with the idea. The city pool was packed with kids, teenagers, and adults, all white, in the pool. Faith was hoping for a lane to do laps but that was hopeless, so she jumped in with her sister and cousins and simply paddled around. The water was refreshing. The city did not heat the pool so it was about twenty degrees cooler than the ambient air. Marion was almost as good a swimmer as her sister. Charles had made sure his girls knew how to swim as soon as they turned four. They were surrounded by lakes, rivers, and the Puget Sound. It just seemed prudent that the girls become strong swimmers.

Faith floated on her back, thinking of the fun family outings to Green Lake. The whole family loved the water, and on those rare July and August days when it was hot in the Northwest, he took them to Green Lake where there was a floating dock.

Nell was posing on the pool edge, hoping Walter noticed her. Rusty and his dad and uncle were playing Marco Polo on the other side of the pool. Faith floated slowly on her back, her eyes closed, thinking of Henry. What was she going to do? She still hadn't seen him or heard from him since the flowers had been delivered last Saturday. She wished she were getting on the next train for home. The thought of another three weeks here made her crazy. *What if I run into him, what if I never hear from him again? How can I go on?*

Her little pity party was rudely interrupted when she was splashed in the face. "Hey, watch it," she said.

Faith looked over and saw a little girl of no more than five thrashing just a few feet to her left. No one seemed to notice her, which was surprising since the pool was so crowded. Marion was floating next to Faith. She rolled over and swam to the child. Marion watched the child go under before she could reach her.

"I've got her," yelled Faith to her sister. She quickly dove to the bottom of the pool. Faith grabbed the listless little girl. She put her arm under the girl's chin and pulled her up with a couple of strong kicks and swam to the side of the pool. The child was a deadweight, and she wasn't sure she could get her out and onto the pool deck. Someone on the side took the child under both arms and dragged her out. Marion pulled herself up. By now a crowd had gathered.

Faith heard a familiar voice say, "Back, everyone, give her some room."

Faith was going to start pumping the child's chest, but before she could climb out of the pool, Henry had bent over the tiny body, his hands on her chest. There was a sputter and then coughing, then crying. He sat her up and someone else gave the child a towel.

She's going to be OK, thought Faith, as she got out of the pool and maneuvered through the people crowded around.

Faith could hear what she guessed was the girl's mother thanking Henry as she headed for the dressing room. Faith did not want to see him, not now.

She quickly showered, dressed, and corralled her amber curls in a purple ribbon. The West Virginia sunshine had brought out thousands of freckles. She was covered from head to foot in them. From a distance it looked like her arms and short legs were a golden tan, but up close it was just a convergence of freckles. Somehow what her Mama told her when she was a little girl, that freckles were the spots the angels left when they kissed her at night, didn't make her happy about them anymore. She looked down at her legs and reflected on her cousin Nell's long ivory limbs. She guessed she was doomed. Both her parents had freckles, both were short, she never had a chance. She walked out to the street looking for a tree with a little shade. She'd just sit and wait for the family. She did feel cooler and in a funny way was grateful to the little girl for taking her mind off Henry, if only for a couple of minutes. She was proud she had rescued her.

She found a tree near the pickup and leaned against the trunk of the old elm as she sat down. She closed her eyes, listening to the laughter from the pool fifty feet away. A breeze had come up and it cooled her freckled skin. It was just enough to lull her into a light sleep.

"Hello, there, Sleeping Beauty."

Faith sat up, rubbed her eyes, and found Henry looking down at her. "Oh, it's you," she said.

"Can I sit down?"

"Suit yourself," said Faith.

"Are you all right? I mean what with the stitches and all." Henry sat, folding his legs in front of him, Indian style. "That was really something you did back there. Everyone wanted to know who it was who dove down and pulled the girl up. Her name is Violet and her mom wants to thank you."

"I guess I just can't help rescuing people," Faith said. She had a twinkle in her eye.

Henry looked at Faith and decided she wasn't going to bite his head off. He smiled back, a little half smile.

"I looked all over for you. So did the rest of your family. Someone saw you leave the dressing room. I told your father that I'd go look for you, and he didn't argue. I think Marion and Rusty were having so much fun that he didn't want to have to make them get out of the pool so soon."

Faith was about to get up, when Henry grabbed her arm. "Let me go, Henry."

"Only if you'll listen to me. I need to apologize for what I said again. I am so sorry, Faith, I really didn't mean it. It just blurted out. I was angry with my father. We had just had another argument over the murder. How could he let Sidney take the fall? All he could say to me was that, if I knew what really happened, I wouldn't want the truth out, either."

Faith sat back down. She could see the pain in his eyes and the anger, too. She leaned over and kissed him on his forehead. She was quick, she didn't want to give him any time to kiss her back, not yet.

"I'm sorry, too," she said. "I better go tell Papa that I'm fine. I don't want him worrying. And I don't want everyone to leave just because of me." She got up and turned toward the pool entrance.

"I'll wait here for you. Hurry back," said Henry.

When Faith got back, Henry had spread a dry towel under the elm. She sat down next to him, but not so close that their bodies touched. She wasn't going to let him off that easy.

"Do you want to talk about it?" she asked him.

Henry nodded. "It's a mess. My mom doesn't even try to put up a front any more. When she's home she locks herself in her bedroom. The old man sleeps in the guest room, and I can hear Mama crying at night. She is so humiliated and ashamed."

They watched some families heading to the parking lot. Faith knew this was hard to talk about. She just sat there quietly with her hands folded in her lap waiting for him to resume.

Finally Henry said, "You know my father was having an affair with Gloria. He admitted it in court and it's been all over the front page of the *Tribune*. He tried to tell me at first that it was a onetime thing, but he couldn't keep that lie up when the headlines said something different. I thought I knew him, but I guess not."

There was no stopping Henry now. It was like the top had popped off a teakettle and the steam was escaping.

"That's not the worst of it, Faith."

Faith just let him get it all out. She listened well. She still didn't say a word. Henry needed no prodding.

"What gets me is that I didn't have a clue that any of this was going on. I'm such a fool."

Now it was Faith's turn. "How could you know? It's not something a father tells his son, after all."

"Mother knew. I know she did. Looking back, it now makes sense that she stopped playing golf with Gloria. Mother also started questioning my father about his hunting trips, and she was always asking him where he was going or where he had been. Why didn't I see it too?"

"Henry, stop it. How could you have known?" Henry put his head in his hands and sighed. "No one but Sidney will have to pay, that's a fact. The trial starts . . ."

Marion came racing up, threw her arms around Faith, and said, "Faith, you're a hero. Everyone's talking about what you did. You saved that little girl! I'm so proud of you."

"Marion, settle down and get hold of yourself. I'm just a natural-born rescuer. Isn't that right, Henry?" She looked at him and smiled. For once she wasn't the one to blush. "I'd better go," she said, as she followed Marion toward the truck. She turned back and said, "The flowers were lovely."

When the family got home, all four children went straight to bed. The sun and the swim had worn them out. All except Faith. She kicked off her covers, rolled over to hear Nell's breathy, dainty snore, and decided it was too muggy to sleep. Besides, her mind was racing about Henry and about the unfairness of the Negro children having no pool where they could cool off.

She went down to the kitchen for a glass of water and found her Papa sitting at the table. He was reading the latest edition of the *Logan Tribune* that he had picked up on the way home from the pool. He turned when he heard footsteps on the stairs. Faith sat down next to him in her nightgown and robe.

"'Having trouble sleeping, Sweet Pea?"

"I think it's so unfair that the Negro boys and girls can't swim in the city pool. And I just can't figure out why Sidney is the only one charged with Mrs. Gannon's murder. I don't think he did it. Do you?"

Charles shook his head.

"It's just the way it is down here. Blacks and whites have always been separated; Negro and white schools, churches, just about everything. Whites don't mix and for the most part, Negroes don't want to mix either."

Faith paused, thought for a moment, and then plunged in. "That's fine and good, but it doesn't get them a pool or even a drinking fountain. Do you think it will ever change?"

Papa looked at her. "No I don't think so, at least not in my lifetime. Folks are used to the way it is."

Faith loved having this alone time with her father and wasn't about to end their conversation. "So who did kill her?"

"I don't know," said Papa. "Maybe it was one of Thompson's doctor friends. It says in the paper that her throat was slit by someone who knew what he was doing. It was a clean cut. Or it could have been her husband. He had a darn good motive. No doubt there's a cover-up, and I do believe Henry's father is mixed up in it somehow."

"What about poor Sidney?" asked Faith.

"He is very loyal to his boss, Henry's dad. My guess is Sidney made a deal to take the fall. Maybe all sixteen of them on Gloria's list got together. Maybe she was blackmailing them. But let's face it, there was blood in the dog car and blood in the basement," said Papa. "Remember there was some kind of get-together there the night of the murder, according to Nell's Aunt Elizabeth. Could have been anyone there."

Faith yawned and began to pick at the place where her stitches had been.

"Let me make you a glass of warm milk. You're never going to get to sleep after this conversation."

He got up and poured milk into a small pan and put it over a warm burner. Even in the heat of the summer, Kitty kept the fire stoked in the stove and just damped it down at night.

"Thanks, Papa. It's all so unfair. I just don't believe a jury will find Sidney guilty."

Papa looked at her and patted her hand. "Be prepared to be disappointed."

TWENTY-FIVE

THE TRIAL WAS SET FOR A week from Monday. Charles made up his mind that he was going.

There were only three weeks left in the Dansworth family's visit to Peach Creek. Charles had mended every fence, built Kitty a new chicken house, cleaned out the basement, and built the Fourth of July stage. The only thing left on Kitty's list was the garage, but Charles wanted to wait for George to help him. He was running out of projects, and he certainly didn't want to be under foot when the canning was in full swing. He'd done his part by bringing all the jars up and getting the shelves ready in the basement. Charles decided that he would be on the courthouse steps an hour before court started and not come home until court was dismissed each day. He would treat it like a job.

He'd always been curious about things and immersed himself in learning about them. When he first came to the logging camp as a teenager, he got a job as a whistle punk. The whistle punk was the kid who blew the whistle when a tree was about to fall. Charles was fascinated by the orchestrated dance the lumbermen performed. Everything about felling an old cedar had to be coordinated closely: the men on the saws, the men on the ropes, the whistle punk, the guys who clipped the limbs and stripped the bark. Charles took it all in and learned everyone's role. He became an expert before he was seventeen. He watched and learned.

Well, he'd watch and learn at Sidney's trial, study all the players, learn who really killed Gloria Gannon, and figure out the motive. The gruesome murder of Gloria Gannon had caught the imagination of all of West Virginia, and it was expected to be the biggest trial in the history of the state. It would be better than a talking picture show, and he was going to have a front-row seat.

TWENTY-SIX

THE FIRST DAY OF THE trial was also the day Sadie and Kitty chose to put up the peaches, the glorious peaches that hung on the trees on Main Street all summer long. Saturday morning the whole neighborhood turned out for the annual peach-picking party, including Faith and the whole family. Men and boys climbed ladders, and small children put the beautiful fruit in wooden crates with something akin to reverence. The women passed out sandwiches and lemonade and icebox cookies. When the trees had been stripped of their bounty, everyone remarked that this was the best crop of Peach Creek peaches in years.

"I think it's because we got that gully washer back in June, right around the time that Gannon woman was found murdered," said an old man in a wide-brimmed straw hat. "And then we've had nothin' but heat. Perfect for growing peaches."

Now the Coles' share of those peaches sat piled up in their boxes out on the back covered porch, the intoxicating fragrance perfuming every room in the house. You could smell peaches from the kitchen to the bedrooms.

"These are the finest peaches we've had in years," said George, peach juice dribbling down his chin. He was headed out the door to work. "Don't forget a thing, Charles," said George, turning to his brother-in-law as he reached the back door. "I want a full account of the trial when I get home tonight. I'll be countin' on you."

Sadie was packing a lunch for Charles. She filled a Mason jar with sweet tea and put it in a lunch pail with two ham-salad sandwiches and a peach and a red-checkered napkin.

Kitty had a huge kettle on the back of the cookstove already coming to a boil to sterilize the jars. She had organized an assembly line of sorts with a station for scalding the peaches to loosen the skin, one for peeling the peaches, one for packing the jars, and one for filling the packed jars with syrup and screwing on the lids. Faith and Nell were finishing their breakfasts, ready to take their places in Kitty's peach line. Every window in the kitchen was flung open to catch the faintest of breezes.

Putting up peaches was a hot endeavor. The stove fires had to be kept hot so the pots would maintain a full boil. This was a precision operation and there was no doubt that Kitty was the general.

"OK, everyone, it's seven o'clock, and our goal is forty-eight jars of Peach Creek peaches cooling on the back porch by eleven this morning. Only a fool would be canning after noon in August," she added. "And I'm no fool. Eat up girls, the syrup is boiling, and we're ready for the first batch. Let's go."

"That's my cue," said Charles. "I'm off to Logan. See you ladies this afternoon."

"Can I go with Papa tomorrow, Mama?" asked Faith.

"Me, too," chimed in Nell.

"Absolutely not," said Kitty and Sadie in unison. Sadie plopped four peaches in the scalding water for about a minute, scooped them out with a slotted spoon, and laid them on the counter to cool so that Kitty could peel, cut, and pit them.

"The courthouse is no place for a lady," said Kitty, as she slipped the skin off a peach, ran a paring knife through it, and popped out the pit in one clean motion. "I don't want you hanging around that place at all this week. There's more than enough to keep you girls busy out here."

"But Mama, everyone's going," said Nell. "All my friends will be there. It's the biggest thing to hit Logan since I don't know what."

"Well, you won't be there," said Kitty. Faith packed five peach halves, each nestled on the top of another, into a wide-mouthed Mason jar, and then slid the jar along the counter to Nell who poured hot syrup over the peaches to the top of the jar, wiped the rim with a damp rag, and screwed on the lid.

"Mama, it's not fair. Can't we at least ride our bikes into town in the afternoon after the canning's done?" said Faith.

"We'll talk about it in the morning, girls," said Kitty. "Right now we've got two crates of peaches waitin' on us, and it's not gettin' any cooler."

Rusty and Marion spent the rest of morning throwing rocks in the creek and hunting for frogs. Marion was convinced that if she saw Broadway she would recognize him. Papa said that if Broadway recognized her he'd hop the other way 'cause he didn't ever want to be cooped up in a shoe box again. After another unsuccessful frog hunt, the cousins came back just in time to listen to the lids pop.

"Music to my ears," said Kitty, wiping her hands on a clean washrag and perusing her finished product. Forty-eight quarts of jewellike peaches were lined up on the back porch.

"There went another one," said Marion.

With every pop, another lid had sealed. There were peaches enough to last the family a whole year.

"When snow fills up the holler and is knee deep in the hills, those peaches will be a reminder of the sweetness of this warm summer day with you," said Kitty, looking at Faith and Sadie and Marion.

"When those jars cool, I want you girls and you, too, Rusty, to cart those jars down to the cellar and place them neat on the shelves right next to the beans. Charles has that basement cleaner than it's ever been and I intend to keep it that way," said Kitty. "And on your way up bring another two dozen jars up. We're putting up cinnamon crab apples tomorrow. I love serving those at Thanksgiving."

Nell and Faith groaned on cue. "How many jars, Ma?" asked Nell.

"Not that many. But I do like to give them out to the neighbors at the holidays. Everyone looks forward to my cinnamon apples. And, just in case you're thinking of something," Kitty said, looking directly at Rusty, "I've hidden the Red Hots."

TWENTY-SEVEN

THE COURTROOM WAS ALREADY PACKED when Charles arrived. The trial wasn't to begin for another hour, but Charles didn't get his front-row seat. In fact he was seated clear in the back, with people still surging through the doors. The courtroom was enormous with wide aisles, high ceilings, and wooden floors shining with layers of shellac, tall windows that opened from the top with a long pole to pull them out. Already the heat was oppressive as more and more people packed in. Soon folks were settled on the side aisles in folding chairs or camping stools that they carried with them. Charles made a note to himself that he would have to leave with George tomorrow to get a better seat. The crowd buzzed, anticipating the first witness of the day. Standing up front on the defendant's side of the room were two fellows Charles remembered from the Fourth of July parade. They had been riding on the sheriff's pickup truck and waving the rebel flag. Charles didn't have a good feeling about them.

At nine o'clock sharp, the bailiff appeared.

"All rise. Court is in session, Judge John Little residing."

As Charles stood, he noticed Sidney Williams and his two prominent attorneys come in and take their seats at the defendant's table. Sidney stared straight ahead. He never looked to his left where those two men stood, but they never took their eyes off him. Both men fidgeted with something in their pockets. Sidney swam in the jail-issued overalls, which had to be rolled up. Beads of sweat stood on his upper lip.

The lawyers for the prosecution took their seats at the table on the other side of the aisle. Judge Little rapped his gavel and court came to order. There was a hush as opening statements were read. The prosecution went first.

"We will prove that on June 21 the defendant, Sidney Williams, brutally murdered and killed Mrs. Gloria Gannon and then dumped her body up on Holden Road on the early morning of June 22. We will show through eyewitness accounts and blood evidence that the defendant acted alone and is the sole perpetrator in this horrific crime."

The defense attorneys, two prominent men from Logan and both on the city council, said the prosecution held the burden of proof and it would become clear through testimony that Mr. Williams had no reason to murder Gloria Gannon, and, furthermore, there were no witnesses to the murder.

And so it went. All morning the state brought witnesses to account for what they knew. The first witness was Mr. Harris of Harris Funeral Home. He testified that he picked up the body of Mrs. Gannon up on Trace Mountain on the afternoon of June 22. "Her body was head down and seemed to be caught in the thicket," he testified. "She was wearing a blue dress with small white dots with some red trim. She was wearing a gold wedding band. She was wearing stockings which had numerous runs in them, but her shoes were missing."

Charles's ears perked up when on cross-examination, the funeral director noted that Gloria had a clean cut from ear to ear on her neck and that her neck was broken. Curiously, there was an index card with a license number placed in a pocket of her dress. Just as curious, no one had found her shoes.

Next Dr. Howard, who examined the body at the funeral home, stated that he thought Mrs. Gannon had been dead seventeen to eighteen hours, and that given the lack of blood at the dump site, her throat had probably been slit at another location. He couldn't tell when the neck had been broken. Maybe before the throat was slit or maybe postmortem, when the body was dumped.

There was a rumbling in the crowd when Officer Gannon took the stand. Folks had been anticipating his testimony. Judge Little lowered his gavel and asked for order. Most of what Gannon said was old news: he was sixteen years older than his wife, knew Sidney for maybe five years, worked the six p.m. to six a.m. shift. Then came the interesting part.

"I called my wife on the morning of June 22 at one thirty in the morning. I was worried about her with all the rain coming down. When I got no answer, I went home and found her bed hadn't been slept in. I called the hospital, but the operator said she hadn't been admitted. At around five in the morning, I went to the Thompsons' and woke up Sidney, who drove me around looking for her."

No one asked why Officer Gannon asked Sidney and not Robert Thompson, his landlord.

All those bodies packed in—there must have been more than three hundred—generated enough heat on their own, and open windows and ceiling fans were not enough to cool the room down. The doors were wide open and Charles was actually happy to be seated near the back where he could feel a little air move.

Judge Little called a lunch recess at eleven thirty, thirty minutes early. Charles left in the first wave and found a spot on the courthouse stairs on the shaded side of the building to eat the lunch Sadie had packed for him. He was amazed at what he saw. Hundreds of people were out in the square waiting for word of what was happening inside. He had never seen that many people at one time in Logan. This trial had taken on a life of its own and it was only day one. Charles took a little note pad and a pencil from his front pocket.

I better write some of this down so I don't forget it. The whole family is gonna want me to report on the happenings, thought Charles.

After an hour and a half for lunch, Officer Gannon's partner, J.J. Danner, told of being with Gannon on the night shift and then of looking for Gannon's wife at around two thirty in the morning, figuring she went missing but not knowing where to look.

"And how did Mr. Gannon decide that Mrs. Gannon was missing," asked the defense lawyer. "What time was it when he reported her missing?"

"Around five o'clock, I reckon, just before his shift ended. He was pretty broken up."

"Well, now. Her body wasn't found till around eleven that morning. Is Mr. Gannon clairvoyant, sir?"

This got a ruffle of laughter from the gallery, and the judge brought his gavel down hard on his oak desk. He asked for order once again.

Shortly before the last witness took the stand there was a ruckus near the front of the courtroom. The bailiff ordered the courtroom cleared as, it seemed, someone was carried from the room. After about a twenty-minute delay, folks began filing back through the doors and took their seats. To Charles, it looked like about fifty people failed to return, probably worn down by the heat of a packed courtroom.

The trial was adjourned at five following the testimony of a well-known colored woman, Rayette Swanson, who ran a boarding house in Logan and took in laundry. She was asked if she ever rented a room to Gloria, and she denied it. The last witness, Oscar James, who was one of Rayette's boarders, stated he saw Mrs. Gannon leaving the boarding house at 8:30 p.m. He overheard two voices talking about seeing each other at the Thompson house later that evening. On cross-examination, James couldn't be sure if either of the voices he heard was that of the murder victim.

Charles was stiff when he got up from the wooden bench he had been sitting on for so long. He felt sweaty all over and took a handkerchief from his breast pocket to wipe his face and neck. He couldn't wait to get back home to his family. The day had taken a toll on him, and he suspected, everyone else in the courtroom, with all the talk of murder, lies, and sex.

Kitty and Sadie were sitting in the rocking chairs on the front porch when he drove up. He was barely out of the truck when the questions began.

"Who was there?" "Did you see Mr. and Mrs. Thompson?" "How'd she look?" "What was she wearing?"

"Whoa," said Charles. His notes were about what the lawyers and witnesses had said. And he hadn't had a chance to even record what had happened after lunch. Nothing about what folks were wearing and who was there. He'd paid no attention to any of that stuff.

"Let's wait till George gets home, and I'll tell you all about the day after supper. I want to go wash up. Judge had to clear the courtroom this afternoon because it was so packed and hot. I think some woman fainted."

Supper was leftovers from Sunday dinner, but was capped off with warm peach cobbler that Nell and Faith had made, in hopes of buttering up their mothers. They were dying to go into Logan Tuesday afternoon just to see what all the excitement felt like.

As Nell said, "Nothing like this has ever happened in Logan County my whole entire life and I'm not about to miss it."

The girls knew that there was no chance that they would be allowed to go into the courthouse for the trial, but they would be content to simply hang around the square in front of it or sit on the steps and wait for Bart Strout to come out and announce the latest news. It was a long shot, they knew, but they were persistent.

"That's mighty good cobbler there, girls. Best I've ever tasted, I do believe," said Charles with a wink in their direction.

"Thanks, Papa. Nell and I were hoping you'd let us go in to Logan after we finish canning tomorrow and maybe get a ride home with you."

Charles tossed a glance in Sadie's direction and saw her give a slight shake of her head "no."

"I'll think it over and talk to your mother and Uncle George and Aunt Kitty. We'll see."

Charles watched as the girls ran up to their room to plan their outfits for the next day. He knew the answer would be no and hated to think about the look of disappointment on their faces when they heard the verdict.

Once Marion and Rusty said their prayers and were tucked in bed, the adults settled on the front porch to listen to the news of the trial.

"Word in the courtroom is that Robert Thompson is scheduled to testify for the prosecution first thing tomorrow morning. Judging by the size of the crowd today, I figure I should leave about the time you take off, George. All right if I get a lift from you? I ended up sitting all the way in the back. It was hard to hear some of the testimony. Only good thing was that I think it was a bit cooler 'cause they left the doors open."

Both Kitty and Sadie gave Charles strict orders for Charles to pay attention to who was seated in the courtroom and what the ladies were wearing. George was more interested in who was tripping up whom.

"I'm thinking this is no place for our girls, Charles," said Sadie.

Kitty chimed in her agreement. "We'll be subjected to whining and pouting, that's for sure, but I don't think they should be in that crowd. If the courthouse was filled today, imagine what it will be like tomorrow. A lot of riffraff down there, I suspect."

Charles nodded in agreement. He'd seen more than a few unsavory characters hanging around, some openly drinking from jars tucked in brown paper bags.

"I'll back you up, but you and Kitty are going to get the brunt of the girls' disappointment. I don't envy you one bit!" said Charles.

Charles was right. He and George told Faith and Nell that they were not to go to Logan and hang around the court-house when the trial was in session.

"We all discussed it after you girls went up to your room, and we concluded that it just isn't a good place for young ladies to be. There are some pretty rough characters around town right now. It just isn't safe."

Charles promised he'd report to them what had happened each day, but, of course, that didn't appease the cousins.

TWENTY-EIGHT

FAITH WAS DETERMINED TO GET to the courthouse, but she had never gone against Papa's orders. It made her feel sick inside, but Faith so wanted to be there for Henry.

The next morning in the kitchen there was no unnecessary conversation, not even any whining. Faith and Nell were all business filling the bottoms of pint jars with a layer of Red Hots and then packing them with tiny, whole crab apples still on their stems, then filling the jars with hot syrup. By eleven, twenty-four bright-red pint-sized jars were lined up on the back porch cooling, all the lids popped and sealed, ready for holiday dinners. There was no point in trying to cheer the girls up. The mood in the kitchen was cold. Kitty didn't bother to ask the girls to help with cleanup after lunch. She and Sadie just wanted them out of sight, so Sadie suggested that they take Marion and Rusty down to Peck's Mill to swim in the afternoon.

"If you want us to," replied Nell, with little enthusiasm.

All morning Rusty and Marion had been trying to stay out of the kitchen and out of the way but had run out of things to do, so they wolfed down their lunches and changed into swimming suits before Faith and Nell were done with their sandwiches.

"Hurry up, you guys," said Rusty, holding a towel and an inner tube.

"OK, OK, we're coming," said Faith.

It took less than twenty minutes to ride their bikes to Peck's Mill, even balancing inner tubes. Most of Peach Creek's population under fifteen was already there. The older boys and a few daring girls took turns swinging from a rope hung from a dogwood tree over the bank.

"If you push off real hard, you can land clear in the middle of the river, but you have to be a strong swimmer to make it to shore, as the current is strong in the center," said Rusty to Marion.

"I'm a stronger swimmer than you," said Marion, as she ran to the rope at the bank's edge.

"Why do we have the strictest parents in Logan County?" complained Nell, spreading a towel on a little sandbar near the shore. "It's not fair. All my friends are at the courthouse today, I just know it."

Faith kept an eye on the younger cousins, as she settled next to Nell. "We have to think of a way to get there, Nell," said Faith. "I need to find Henry and see how he's holding up. Papa said Henry's father might be testifying today."

"I thought you weren't speaking to Henry ever again," said Nell.

"I don't know how I feel. When we talked on Monday outside the pool, I think he really was sorry about what he said to me. He apologized again and said he had just had a big argument with his father at the bank, when he ran into me. I kind of believe him."

"Did you let him kiss you?"

"Absolutely not!" said Faith.

She didn't tell her cousin that she had kissed Henry on the top of his head, however. Some things needed to be just between her and Henry. She wasn't totally sure of her own feelings, so she wasn't going to share everything with her cousin.

"How are we going to get out of the house tomorrow and get to Logan without the canning queens finding out?"

Nell laughed. "What if we said that we wanted to see Cecelia?"

"Maybe that will work, but you do the talking. I can't lie worth beans. My ears turn red," said Faith.

Nell and Faith spent the rest of the afternoon scheming about their big escape. They would tell their mothers that they ran into Cecelia today and she asked them to come over tomorrow for lunch. It was perfect. Kitty and Sadie had talked that morning about going to sewing circle tomorrow afternoon in Peach Creek, so they wouldn't be anywhere to check on them. By the time the plans were laid, both girls were in a much better mood and even took a few swings on the rope. It really did feel refreshing to plunge into the cool water. On the way home, they stopped at Richard's Creamery.

"Go ahead and pick two flavors each," said Nell, as she pulled her wallet from her swim bag. "My treat."

She and Faith had double-deckers, too. They all sat on the curb in front of the Peach Creek ice cream parlor and ate the cool treats fast before the ice cream melted down their hands.

TWENTY-NINE

IN TOWN, CHARLES ARRIVED AT the courthouse and was admitted with the first wave of observers. It was another hot day. The forecast for the week showed no signs of a cooling trend, and Charles noted that all the windows and doors were already flung wide open, as he took a seat in the fourth row. A heavy fellow, with a plug of tobacco that made his left cheek bulge out and dark stains from heavy sweating under his armpits, slid along the bench next to Charles.

"Morning." Charles nodded to the stranger. Stale sweat wafted from the fellow, and Charles wondered if he could last the day sitting next to him.

There was a rumbling at the entrance doors as people shoved past the sheriff's deputies trying to get good seats. The rumor that Robert Thompson would be on the stand for the state this morning had brought a bigger crowd, just as Charles had predicted.

"So, do you think the nigger killed her?" asked the odorous man.

"No," said Charles. "It's all a setup if you ask me."

"Doesn't matter. He had no business messin' with a white woman. I hope they hang the boy." Tobacco juice dribbled out of the side of his mouth as he spoke. Charles edged as far down the bench as possible.

The first few people called to the stand for the prosecution dealt with timetables and establishing the whereabouts of Sidney, Mr. Thompson, and other people involved in the murder and investigation. The temperature in the courtroom was steadily rising, and people were fanning themselves with fans passed out by Harris Funeral Home.

Now there's a clever piece of advertising, thought Charles.

Charles thought of his daughter. She knew sentiment ran to convicting Sidney, yet she still held firm in her belief that he was innocent and justice would prevail. Charles was glad she wasn't here to listen to this fool next to him, whose sentiment was sadly shared by most every white person in the courthouse. The colored in the balcony felt differently.

At about eleven in the morning, Robert Thompson was called to the stand. The courtroom started buzzing. Judge Little rapped his gavel for the first time that day. Thompson testified again about his affair with Gloria and admitted to it lasting over two years. Hazel Thompson sat in the front row staring straight ahead, shoulders squared, back straight. Charles noted (for the wives) that she wore a little blue hat perched at an angle. There was a brown pheasant feather that never moved. He could only imagine her pain and humiliation as she listened to her husband's testimony.

"And how did the two of you get together?" asked the attorney for the defense on cross-examination.

"Well, usually Sidney Williams, my handyman, would bring her to a place, like my hunting cabin up on Holden Road, and then drop her at Holden 21 Store, and she'd get a taxi home. I tried to get her home by eleven. I think that was her curfew."

Snickers could be heard from the other attorneys at the defense table as well as from the crowd. The gavel came down hard this time along with a warning from the judge for no more outbursts or he would clear the courtroom.

The man next to Charles leaned over and spoke in Charles's ear. Charles could not only smell his hot breath, he could also feel it and practically taste it. He slid away from him as far as he could manage.

"Seems like every bloke in Logan was gettin' some nooky from that Gloria dame. How come I didn't get a turn?"

It was a welcome relief when Judge Little called for the lunch recess a little after noon. When Charles returned he vowed to sit as far away from his current seatmate as possible.

The afternoon was filled with technical testimony from the state lab in Charleston regarding blood. It was noted that the cut was very clean and precise. Nothing was said that hadn't already been reported in the *Tribune* two weeks earlier. The twelve men in the jury box looked bored and sleepy. One man's head bobbed and jerked as he woke himself up. Sweat beaded up on many an upper lip and brow. It was a relief when the judge adjourned court early.

When Charles sat down to supper Tuesday evening with the family, he noted a change; Nell and Faith were in a markedly better mood.

"Nell bought us double-decker ice-cream cones today," said Marion. "And we got to go to Peck's Mill to swim."

"Why this sudden burst of generosity, Nell?" asked George.

"No reason."

"So what are you gals puttin' up tomorrow?" asked Charles.

"We're taking a break," said Sadie. "We thought we'd go to Ladies Sewing Circle. We're making quilts for the orphans in China. Pastor Corn heard Pearl Buck speak at the Baptist convention in Charleston last month and got everyone excited about her charities.

"Cecelia said she won the Pulitzer Prize for her book this year," said Faith. "And guess what? She was born in West Virginia."

"And what are you children up to?" said George, looking directly at Nell. She stared right back.

"Faith and I are going to have lunch with Cecelia. Mother said Rusty and Marion are going with them to Circle so they can play with Mrs. Adams's kids. Right, Mama?"

Faith fiddled with her beans and never looked up.

THIRTY

THURSDAY MORNING CHARLES HEADED OUT early with George. The plan was to drop his brother-in-law off at the rail yard at the Front and then get a prime spot at the courtroom for day three.

"So what do you expect today?" asked George.

"Word has it that the prosecution will rest and the defense will begin. Not sure if Sidney will testify or not, but he's got some damn fine lawyers, that's for sure," said Charles. "I find it bewildering how a colored fellow charged with murdering a white woman gets these high-powered fellows to defend him."

"Not to mention all that food sent over from the Smokehouse Restaurant. Pretty clear there's a deal between Sidney and one or more of the big guns on that mysterious list Gloria made. Sure would like to get my hands on that thing," said George.

"You and most of the town," said Charles. "What do you think those girls are up to? I smell something fishy."

"Me, too. I know they're hell-bent to get into town and see what's goin' on. Do you really think it's dangerous?"

"Judging from what I saw yesterday, starting with that character I sat next to all morning, I'd say damn right it's dangerous. It's definitely no place for those two to be wandering around. This whole thing will be over by the end of the week, and then things will settle down."

"If we can hold the girls down that long. "

THIRTY-ONE

"Do you think we should really go to your Aunt Elizabeth's? I'm getting nervous about this whole plan."

"Come on, Faith. I know you want to be there. It was your idea. Maybe you'll see Henry."

"Of course I want to be there, but I'm no good at lying. What if we actually go and get Cecelia? That way we could at least say we went where we said we would. It wouldn't really be lying that way."

"All right I guess, but let's get going. I don't want to get into it with Mama," said Nell, brushing her long black hair and tying it back with a purple grosgrain ribbon. She took one last glance in the mirror and followed Faith out the door and down the stairs.

"Bye, Mama," she called.

Faith did the same, hoping neither woman would come out of the kitchen.

When they got to Logan they rode their bikes directly to Aunt Elizabeth's as agreed upon. Elizabeth opened the massive oak door and looked at her unexpected guests.

"What a nice surprise," she said. "Does Cecelia know you girls are coming?"

"No, but we haven't seen her in a while, and everyone will be going back home in a week," said Nell, a visible look of sadness on her face.

Faith, once again dazzled by the crystal chandelier in the foyer and the elegant parlor beyond, didn't even notice Cecelia coming down the winding staircase.

"Hi, Nell. Hello, Faith," said Cecelia. "What a nice a surprise to see you both."

Cecelia led the girls into the parlor, with its brick fireplace that was large enough to stand in. This was where Faith had been hit with the brick and had woken up on the horsehair sofa. "Come with us. We're going to the five-and-dime for lunch," said Nell. No mention was made of going to the courthouse.

Maybe Nell's right not to mention it, thought Faith. There'd be time to explain things at lunch.

"Can Cecelia take a walk with us? We thought we'd go to the dime store for flapper Cokes and maybe a sandwich or something," asked Nell, when her Aunt Elizabeth walked in the room.

Aunt Elizabeth hesitated.

"Please, Aunt Liz," pleaded Nell.

"I'm surprised your folks let you ride into town with the trial going on and all, but I guess it can't hurt," Elizabeth said, "as long as you go straight there and come right back. The poor girl has been cooped up with Morris and me for several days. No more parties to plan."

The girls left their bicycles on Elizabeth's expansive porch and walked to Logan's central square directly in front of the courthouse.

"I thought we were going to the five-and-dime," said Cecelia.

"We will, but this is the biggest thing that's ever happened in my lifetime, and I'm not about to miss it," said Nell.

They were elbow to elbow with other residents of the county. Families had camp stools and baskets of food. Little children were everywhere. Some were staying close to their mamas, but others were running amuck, climbing the chestnut trees lining the courthouse square, chasing each other, some of the more unruly ones punching each other and even biting. Young men leaned against the courthouse, smoking or chewing and spitting.

"Do you recognize anyone here?" asked Faith.

"Not so far, but let's walk around a bit. Maybe we'll see someone we know."

A couple of unsavory-looking older boys shared drinks out of a paper bag. They whistled catcalls at the cousins, looking them up and down slowly as the girls hurried by.

"Keep walking and look straight ahead," said Faith, as one of boys reached out to grab her arm.

"Want a drink, ladies?" one of them shouted after them.

Even Nell was beginning to think this might not be a good idea. "Let's get a Coke," she said.

The lunch counter was full, but it was already one o'clock and most of the diners were eager to get back to the courthouse. Just as they were about to be seated, Faith spotted her father at the end of the counter. Pointing to him and putting her fingers to her lips, she motioned Nell and Cecelia to follow.

"Hurry!" she whispered.

The girls stood huddled behind a display rack of lotions and creams. It was just blind luck that Charles didn't spot his daughter and the other two girls as they ducked down. Neither Faith nor Nell had factored in a court recess when they were planning their big escape. Sadie had packed him a lunch the last couple of days. Why was he here?

"Oh, my gosh!" whispered Nell. "Uncle Charles would kill us if he saw us here."

"What are you talking about, Nell?" asked Cecelia.

"We aren't allowed to come downtown until the trial is over. We're only allowed to go to see you and then straight home. Our parents think it's way too dangerous," said Nell. "Can you believe it?"

Faith hadn't said a word. She was shaking and her heart was pounding in her chest. She was sure it must be visible. The guilt was palpable. She swallowed hard. Finally she spoke.

"Maybe we should get out of here, go back to Cecelia's like we said we were doing."

"Come on, Faith. We just got here. Let's at least have lunch and then we can go right back to Cecelia's." Nell poked her head up over the creams. "The coast is clear, come on."

Faith realized her chance of finding Henry was remote, and she was feeling uncomfortable after their encounter with those boys by the courthouse.

"We're already here. Let's just check things out for a while after we finish," said Nell. "What do you want to do, Cecelia?"

"Let's eat and then decide," was her reply.

So they ate their pimento-cheese sandwiches and drank their flapper Cokes and went out in the square again. The crowd was even larger than before. Nell found a few high-school friends and wanted to talk, but Faith and Cecelia didn't recognize anyone they knew except Walter and a girl named Dorothy.

"Let's get out of here," said Cecelia.

Cecelia began to bite her nails and shift from one foot to the next. There was an uneasiness in the air. Faith saw more men drinking from paper bags, and it felt like a fight could break out any minute.

"I don't think it's safe around here. Papa was right, there's riffraff everywhere," said Faith. "Cecelia and I are heading back. I wish you'd come, too, but I know you won't. Be careful."

"I will," said Nell. "I'll meet you at Aunt Elizabeth's in an hour, I promise."

Cecelia and Faith were glad to get out of there. By now three boys from school were buzzing around Nell, and Faith knew there was no way her cousin would leave. Swinging her hair with a flick of her head, Nell waved to them. "See you later," she called.

Faith and Cecelia walked quickly back to Aunt Elizabeth's. Thankfully, it was only three blocks away.

"Where's Nell?" asked Elizabeth, when they got home. She looked concerned.

"She ran into some friends from school and wanted to talk, so we agreed to meet back here in an hour," said Cecelia, trying to reassure her aunt. "Don't worry, Aunt Liz. She's just a couple of blocks away, and they were all sitting on the benches in the main square. She's fine."

The two girls settled into the couches in the parlor and began talking books. Cecelia always had a book with her; Faith shared her love for reading.

"The Chinese woman who's the main character in *The Good Earth* has such a miserably hard life. Women in China have absolutely no freedom. You've got to read it—it's amazing. You can borrow my copy."

The grandfather clock in the corner bonged one . . . two . . . three . . . four. Faith looked at Cecelia.

"Nell should be here by now. She's at least fifteen minutes late and we need to be home by four thirty. Otherwise Mama and Aunt Kitty will beat us home. Papa has been getting back from the trial around five, and that's when Uncle George gets off work. We're cutting it close."

When Nell still wasn't back at five, everyone was concerned. Elizabeth sent out her husband Morris to look for her.

"Let me go, too," said Faith.

"OK," said Morris, "But don't go running off on your own. I don't want two lost gals on my hands."

They walked the perimeter of the courthouse square, then down Stratton Street as far as the *Tribune* offices. They looked in the bakery, the drugstore and the Smokehouse Restaurant, but no luck.

"What was she doing downtown by herself anyway?" asked Morris.

"She met up with some friends after lunch, and Cecelia and I decided to go home. She said she'd be home by four."

"Well, this surely isn't the place for Nell to be by herself, especially with the trial going on," said Morris.

They decided to take one more trip around the courthouse yard. Most of the crowd was gone. There were just a few unsavory fellows hanging around. Faith didn't want to let Morris know it, but she was beginning to panic.

What if we can't find her? What if she somehow got mixed up with those men drinking moonshine? thought Faith. Wild scenarios played out in her mind, none of them good.

Morris rubbed his temples. "I think I'd better take you back and then try to find Charles. Maybe he'll have a better idea of where to look."

Faith could feel her heart jump in her chest. She grabbed Morris's shirtsleeve. "Please, let's just look a little longer. I'm sure Nell will turn up." Her voice was not convincing.

Morris wasn't buying it. "I don't like this, Faith. It's dangerous out here, and the courthouse is almost empty. There are too many fellows who've been drinkin' all day. And it'll be dark soon. Let me take you back and get your dad."

As they walked the two blocks home, Faith was so scared she could barely breathe. She was actually more worried about what had happened to Nell than the wrath that would come down on them when their parents found out they had lied and come to the courthouse square. They climbed the porch steps, and Morris pulled the grand front door open for them. Nell was standing there as if nothing had happened, all excited about her afternoon adventures.

"Where were you? We were scared half to death. We're gonna get killed when we get home." Faith's face was flushed and her ears blazed red and she didn't care. "You can do the explaining. I'm not going to cover for you."

"Oh, for gosh sake, Faith, settle down. You're such a scaredy-cat. Let's go."

Without even an apology or a thank you, Nell walked out the door and down to her bike and took off. Faith could hardly contain her fury.

I wish I were home, she thought. *I've had it with Nell and her sneaking around. And all for nothing. I didn't even get a glimpse of Henry.*

Faith peddled hard to keep up with Nell, whose long legs propelled her forward with half the effort. Only one more week with Nell, then they would board the train back to Seattle. And only one week until Henry went off to Marshal.

The fall semester didn't begin until mid-September, but Henry was on a football scholarship and had to report three weeks early for practice. Faith hadn't seen or talked to him since the pool incident. *Did he even want to see her again?* She was riding faster and faster trying hard to keep up with Nell. Sweat dripped from her forehead and her dress was sticking to her back. She began to cry, and the salt from her tears burned her eyes and made it hard to see. *I'm a mess. My life is a mess.*

Faith and Nell were met at the front door by the whole family. "You're in big trouble," said Rusty, letting out a long low whistle.

Charles and George stood with their arms crossed. "Morris just left. He drove over to tell us you girls were at the courthouse and that you couldn't find Nell," said Charles to both girls.

George looked at Nell who had a defiant look in her eyes. "Don't be so unreasonable, Papa," said Nell. "All I did was hang out with friends from school for an hour. Nothing bad happened, I just lost track of time."

Kitty chimed in. "Sadie and I were under the impression that you were going to Elizabeth's to have lunch with Cecelia. And we specifically told you not to go near the courthouse. If we had thought that you'd be gallivanting all over Logan, we certainly wouldn't have given you permission to go."

Neither Nell nor Faith was very hungry, and no one objected when they asked to be excused from the supper table.

Faith was furious with her cousin and Nell knew it.

"Come on, Faith. I really didn't mean to be late. It's just that Walter actually asked me out. He wants me to go with him to the kick-off dance for our senior year. I couldn't just brush him off."

"But you could brush me off," said Faith. "Didn't it ever cross your mind how much trouble you'd get us in? Obviously not, given the predicament we're now in."

"That's not fair, Faith. You wanted to go, too, and you know it."

Faith replied, "Maybe a little, but I didn't get us caught and then stuck in the house my last week here. And, by the way, you'll be lucky if you get to go to the dance. I'll bet Aunt Kitty won't let you leave the house till you graduate."

Nell laughed, and despite her best efforts, Faith couldn't help but join her. It was hard to stay mad at Nell for long.

Faith was right. Their folks doled out their punishment.

"Neither of you are allowed to leave the house for a week. That means you will absolutely not go to Logan for any reason. No swimming at Peck's Mill, no picture shows, no nothing," said George.

"What if people want to visit us here?" asked Nell, always looking for an angle.

"I'll think about it," said George.

THIRTY-TWO

IT WAS SATURDAY, DAY ONE of the imposed punishment. Nell and Faith were finishing up the breakfast dishes when there was a knock at the door. Marion answered and yelled to the kitchen, "Faith, it's your boyfriend."

"Marion!" said Faith. She dried her hands on her apron and tried to smooth her unruly hair. She bit her lips a few times and pinched her cheeks in hopes of brightening up her appearance.

I'm a mess, she thought. She hung the apron on a hook by the stove and walked out to meet Henry.

It had been more than a week since she and Henry had seen each other at the pool. Henry stood barely inside the front door, dressed in a freshly ironed plaid cotton shirt and khaki pants. It was as if Faith were seeing him for the first time. He was so handsome it took her breath away. She wanted to run her hands through his sandy-blond hair and push it back where it had fallen over one blue eye.

"Hello, Faith," said Henry. "I was hoping I'd catch you at home. Can you take a walk with me up the hill?"

Charles was on the porch.

"Can I, Papa?"

"You know the rules. You're not to leave this house for a week."

"Please, Papa. We won't be gone long, and we won't go far. I'll even make sure the house is in view."

"Oh, all right, but just for a little while."

"Give me a minute," said Faith. She gave Marion a look that said, *"If you say one word, I'll kill you."*

She ran upstairs and quickly changed into her blue gingham dress with the white piping on the sweetheart collar. She felt pretty in it. She tied a ribbon around her hair and dabbed on a little lipstick. When she reappeared, Henry was talking to Marion about frogs, and Marion didn't even notice that Faith had changed outfits and added lipstick.

"Ready?" she asked.

Henry took a butterscotch candy from his pocket and tossed it to Marion. "Here, good lookin'."

Marion caught the candy and actually had trouble saying thank you, she was so flustered.

Looks like Henry has stolen Marion's heart, too, thought Faith.

They walked up the road past the Methodist church and began to follow the creek up into the hills, but not as far as where Nell got bit by the copperhead. Henry took Faith's hand, but neither of them spoke. There was a small clearing next to the creek where it curved to the right ever so slightly and a sandbar reached out to the water. Faith couldn't see the Cole house, but she figured no one would come looking for them. She loved the now-familiar sound of the water spilling over the flat rocks that didn't quite drown out the cacophony of birdcalls from the overhanging hickory and dogwood trees. Nature even supplied a log to lean against. Faith looked around, listened to the sounds, and breathed in the piney scent from the trees up the hill. She wanted to remember this place. To her it represented the best of Peach Creek. She now understood why the hills and hollers were so precious to the people in these parts. Mother Nature had outdone herself. It wasn't the spectacular view from her apartment window in Seattle, where on a clear day Mt. Rainier came out of the shroud of clouds and mist to appear as if on a postcard. This view was intimate and close and always available. You just had to walk up to it.

"Do you want to sit down?" asked Henry.

Faith arranged her skirt under her and leaned back into the old elm log. Henry sat down beside her. Their arms and thighs touched and a shiver ran through Faith clear to her toes. Henry took her hand in his hands and said, "I've missed you, Faith."

"I've missed you, too."

Henry leaned over and kissed her. She kissed him back.

"This isn't exactly 'spin the bottle,'" Faith quipped, hoping to lighten the moment before things got to the point of no return.

Henry laughed and sat up. Faith did the same, straightening her clothes.

"I really did bring you up here to talk," he said. "I leave next Friday for Marshall and have so much to tell you. The trial is taking so much time, and now I have to help pack up the house."

"Why?"

"I thought you knew. Everyone in these parts seems to know all our family business. Dad took a position in the capital at Charleston National Bank. Mother sat in the courthouse when my father testified, but she hasn't left her room since. Father is hoping the change will help. Maybe it will. I don't know, though. I think the scandal will follow them."

Henry took out a handkerchief and wiped his forehead. "I'm just glad that I have college and won't have to come back here. I haven't got many friends left." He looked sad.

"I'm so sorry for all of this," she said.

"It's OK, really. The worst is over. I don't know what else anyone could say that could be worse than what's been in the paper."

He took off his shoes and socks and dug his feet in the sand. "Come on. Let's wade in the creek."

"We should head back pretty soon. I promised Papa."

But Faith took her shoes and stockings off, too, showing her bare legs covered in freckles. Henry pulled her up, and they ventured out onto the flat rocks in front of them. Henry leapt over to the largest one in the middle, holding out his hand for Faith to follow him. She stayed in the shallow water letting the coolness splash over her ankles and feet.

"Come on out and sit with me on the rock," said Henry.

Faith waded further out. The water was almost to her knees as she gingerly stepped between rocks. Henry held out his hand. She took hold and held her skirt up in her other hand. He pulled her up, but not enough. Her bare foot slipped on the slimy rock, and she fell backward. Henry couldn't help himself as he watched Faith sputter and splash. She was totally submerged, her dress clinging to her body, her hair dripping. She watched helplessly as the ribbon holding her hair drifted downstream. Henry tried to hide his amusement but it was hopeless. His whole body shook with laughter.

"You stop that, Henry Thompson, and help me up!"

Henry slid from the rock and gathered Faith around the middle. Faith was aware of his long body pressed against her. She should have been furious, but she began to laugh with him. It felt so good to just give in to the whole thing. And she didn't want Henry to let go. They stood in the middle of the small creek and let the water move around them.

"Are you cool enough now?" laughed Henry.

Faith smacked him on his arm.

"Look at me. What will Mama say? I'm getting out of this creek so my clothes can dry."

With that she treaded very carefully to the sandbar and wrung out a bucket of water from her skirt.

"Why don't you let me hang your things over a tree branch to dry?" teased Henry.

"Henry Thompson! I might as well plan my funeral. What if Marion and Rusty come up looking for us? Good lord, I shudder to think."

Henry threw back his head and let out a whistle. "You don't have to take off your clothes. I'm enjoying the sight."

For some reason this didn't embarrass Faith. She liked Henry looking at her. He made her feel safe and he made her feel almost beautiful, even as she felt her hair dry into tight curls in the sun.

"I hate the idea of not being able to see you," said Faith.

"It'll be OK. We can write and maybe you can come out next summer. And there are telephones. I'll save my money so I can call you. Besides we've got one more week."

Faith had thought of all of this already. It didn't help. There would be a whole continent between them, and she knew Papa would never let her come across the country alone, but she didn't want to spoil the morning so she smiled and sat down on the log, spreading her skirt out to dry. It took no time for the sun to do its trick. Both she and Henry were happy to be sitting side by side alone in the woods.

Faith broke the mood, at last. "What do you want me to do with the shoe? It's still in my grip in the back of Nell's closet. What do you think happened to the other one? It seems strange that they both weren't there."

"I don't think an old shoe will help anyone. Can you put it in a paper bag when we get back? I'll take it to Marshall with me and throw it away there. Then there's no way anyone from around here will find it."

"I don't know, Henry. That shoe is evidence, and I think you should have turned it over to the sheriff's office. It's not too late."

"Faith!"

There was no mistaking that voice. She saw Marion running up the hill toward them with Rusty in tow.

Marion was breathless. "Mama says you two have been up here long enough and you need to get back for lunch. Henry, you are invited to stay if you want."

"I'd love to, Cutie-pie."

Faith rarely saw Marion blush, but the telltale rosy ears were a giveaway. *It must be a Dansworth curse*, Faith thought.

"Did you guys fall in the creek?" asked Rusty. Their clothes were nearly dry but sand stuck in the folds of the wrinkled fabric.

"Mama's gonna kill you," said Marion. "She's none too happy that you have been up here with your boyfriend for so long."

"How 'bout a nickel for each of you if you run ahead and tell your mother that Faith and I are on our way?" said Henry, reaching into his pocket for a couple of coins. "And after lunch we can walk down to the creamery for ice cream while Faith gets back in her mother's good graces."

He handed the two children their money and winked at Faith. When they were out of sight and earshot, Henry gave Faith another quick kiss and then brushed the sand from her backside.

"We're just going to have to tell the truth that you slipped on a rock and I fell in trying to pull you up. They don't need to know all the details."

With that, Faith gathered up her stockings and slipped on her shoes over her bare feet. Henry took her hand and they walked in silence following the lovely little creek down the hill.

Henry charmed Sadie just as he had her daughters.

"You could make shoe leather taste delicious, Mrs. Dansworth. I bet there are lines around the block at Broadway Lunch with folks waiting to get a taste of your fine cooking."

Henry even offered to wash up the dishes, but Marion and Rusty quickly reminded him of the ice cream, so Sadie sent them off with Henry for ice-cream cones. After lunch, the house was empty except for Faith and her mother.

Charles and George decided to tackle the garage. It was the last thing left on Kitty's list, and Charles wanted to cross it off before they left for Seattle in just a week. Kitty and Nell had more clothes to leave at the post office for the Widows Relief Fund.

"He's a nice boy, Faith," Sadie said, as she and Faith finished up the dishes in the kitchen. "You're going to miss him, aren't you?"

Faith was a little surprised that her mother wasn't upset with her for spending such a long time alone with Henry this morning. Faith had noticed a real change in her mother over the last month. She smiled more and wasn't as critical. When she and Nell snuck off to Logan during the trial, it was Papa, not Mama, who brought down the hammer. Mama actually came to their defense. "Kitty and I did give them permission to go to see Cecelia. In retrospect we shouldn't have let them go," she had told Charles.

Sadie took off her apron and poured two glasses of sweet tea. "Let's go sit out on the porch and wait for Henry and the children to get back."

Faith was surprised at the invitation but pleased. They settled in the rocking chairs, sitting side by side, Sadie in the wooden one with the beautifully curved back and wide arms polished to a shine from all the hands that had rested there. Faith sat in the soft, pillowy brown leather one. The house was so quiet with just the two of them alone on the porch. Sadie took a sip of tea and set it down on a little yellow iron table between them. "Faith, I have an apology to make."

Faith looked genuinely startled.

"Just listen to me and don't say anything," said Sadie to her daughter. "I'm sorry that I haven't been the mother I should have been to you and your sis. Things are going to change. Papa and I have decided to hire an extra person for after school, so you won't have to work."

Faith didn't know what to say, so she just sat there and rocked.

Sadie continued, "After Becky died, I just couldn't get over the sadness. The world looked so dark. I'm so ashamed."

Faith stood up and put her arms around her mother. For the first time in her life, it felt like she and her mother were equals and that Sadie was talking to Faith like an adult. It felt good.

"Thank you, Mama, but I don't mind working after school."

Mama took a breath and held Faith's hand. "There's something I want you to know. I haven't even told Kitty yet . . ."

A look of apprehension crossed over Faith's face.

"Oh, Honey, it's good news. I'm going to have a baby."

"How?"

Sadie burst out in laughter, watching as Faith turned beet red when she realized what she had just asked.

Just then Rusty bounded up the steps ahead of Marion and Henry.

"Look, Aunt Sadie, Henry bought us triple-deckers!"

Marion was walking right next to Henry, chocolate ice cream dripping down her chin.

"There's no denying my baby sister has a bad case of puppy love," said Faith to her mother, careful not to let Rusty hear her comment. She knew that Rusty would tease Marion mercilessly if he heard Faith, but right now he was so engrossed in eating the triple-decker that he didn't notice anything else.

"She won't be your baby sister for long," said Mama with a smile. "Let's keep the news our little secret for a while."

THIRTY-THREE

THE IMPOSED HOUSE ARREST, AS Nell called it, turned out to be a blessing in disguise. It was almost as if Faith and Nell were holding court, so many people came by to see them.

As the week progressed, Faith finished *The Good Earth* and spent a wonderful afternoon with Cecilia talking about the horrible plight of women in China. "In some ways, the miners' families are as oppressed as the women in China," said Cecelia. "They have so little hope and no way to improve their lives."

"I don't think it's quite that bad," said Nell. "At least we don't bind girls' feet."

"I've decided that I don't want to get married," said Cecelia. "I'm going to become a Baptist missionary and go to China."

"How do you think your parents will feel about that?" asked Nell. "You're their only child. Do you really think they'd let you travel all the way to China? I hope I fall in love and get married, maybe next year if I'm lucky, and have a passel of babies. And I can't imagine ever leaving Logan County."

"I don't know, Nell. I can see Cecelia's point of view," said Faith. "I can't picture myself married anytime soon. I am going to the University of Washington, and then I want to see the world. Maybe I'll visit Cecelia in China. Maybe I'll be a writer like Pearl Buck. You never know.

"Oh, come on, Faith. Are you telling me you'd turn Henry down if he asked you to marry him?" asked Nell.

"He'd just have to wait," said Faith.

Cecelia chimed in, "Look at Faith's Aunt Alma. She's got a perfectly wonderful life and she never married."

Faith added, "She's so darned independent. I love that about her."

"Well, I sure don't want to be an old maid," huffed Nell.

When I left Seattle I had never had a boyfriend, and here I am in love and, amazingly, not wanting to get married any time soon, Faith thought.

It was true. This charming, exasperating place had opened her eyes and expanded her possibilities.

Henry was an almost daily visitor. During the day, he was busy packing up the family home for their move to Charleston, but he came in the early evening, always spending time with the whole family. Rusty quizzed him on all things football and Henry taught him how to throw a perfect spiral.

With only five days before Henry was leaving for Huntington and Marshall College, he told Faith, "I don't want you to come to the Front to see me off. I promise I'll come by Thursday night to say good-bye. My folks leave Friday, too, and I don't think I can take all those good-byes in one day. Besides your big going-away party is that night, and you'll be busy getting ready for it."

It was true that Friday would be busy. Besides the party and packing for home, the trial should be wrapping up. Papa went faithfully every day to the courthouse, and ever since the episode with Nell, he let Faith and Nell sit in on his nightly reports.

"This way our parents can be sure we won't sneak off again," said Nell.

Faith didn't say it out loud, but there was no way she would go back into Logan while the trial was going on. She had found out firsthand that it really was the scary place that her parents had warned them of. She could still feel that drunk man's hand on her arm and it gave her the shivers.

Papa had expected the trial to be over by now, but the defense brought on a lot more people to testify than anyone expected. Faith thought this was a good sign. Maybe Sidney would be acquitted after all. Papa said that all the testimony was circumstantial. No one could place Sidney with Gloria Gannon. There were no eyewitnesses. Closing arguments were scheduled for Thursday and then it would go to the jury that afternoon.

"I have a feeling we'll have a verdict sometime this Friday," said Papa. "I hope we do 'cause I would hate to have sat through the whole bloody thing and not know the outcome. They won't deliberate over the weekend and we leave Saturday."

Aunt Kitty invited Elizabeth, Morris, Ralph, and Cecelia out for dinner Wednesday night.

"I wanted to have you here one last time before everyone leaves. Besides, it will be hard to visit at the party Friday night. I think we've invited half the population of Logan County," said Kitty.

After dinner, Cecelia handed Faith a package wrapped in bright green paper with a huge silver ribbon.

"You didn't need to bring me a present, Cecelia. It's so pretty, I hate to open it."

"You must," said Cecelia.

Inside was a fine red leather diary with Faith's name stamped in gold. Faith had never owned something so precious, and she didn't know quite what to say.

"It's so you can put down all your hopes and dreams. I believe if you write them down they are more likely to come true," said Cecilia.

"Oh, it is perfect," said Nell with not the least bit of jealousy.

The next morning, Faith got up early to do laundry and begin packing.

"I'm about to cry crocodile tears," said Nell, as she watched her cousin fold the yellow voile dress in tissue paper and put it in the bottom of her grip with Aunt Alma's beaded evening bag. "It will feel like a funeral parlor around here without you and your family. I'll die of boredom. You have to promise to write every day, and I'll do the same. Maybe Papa will let me call you on the phone once in a while. I know it's expensive, but we can't lose touch. We are kindred spirits now, Faith."

Faith recalled how in June these long soliloquies of her cousin gave her a headache. Now Faith saw them as a most endearing quality. She would miss Nell dearly, as well as Rusty, Uncle George, and Aunt Kitty, and all the wonderful people she had met this summer. She had kin and now she really knew them. She knew in her heart she belonged to these wonderful Peach Creek relatives. They were family.

THIRTY-FOUR

"Look, the leaves on the peach trees are beginning to turn. It seems too early," said Faith.

"Not really," said Henry. "It will be September in just a couple of days."

They both looked out at the trees in the fading twilight. The bamboo supports were gone, stored away for next year's harvest. The limbs hung high with all the peaches stripped from the trees. It was a beautiful evening. The frog melody blended with the rustle of the leaves. It mixed with the faint sound of water as it trickled over the rocks in Peach Creek across the road. A harvest moon the size of a prized county-fair pumpkin hung heavy in the sky. Faith closed her eyes as she tried to imprint the scene in her memory. She had never been this happy and this melancholy at the same time, and she wanted to remember this moment forever.

A tiny shudder rippled through Faith's body as Henry took her hand. He had come over a little early this Thursday afternoon so he could spend time with Marion and Rusty, too. Marion drew him a picture of herself to take to his dorm room.

"It's me, so you won't forget what I look like," she said, handing him a folded-up paper.

"It's a fine rendering, Marion. I promise to put it on my bulletin board and tell all my new college friends about what a fine girl you are," he said, as Marion turned rosy.

Rusty made Henry pinky swear that he would send Rusty a pennant from Marshall. They played catch before supper, while Faith helped in the kitchen. Aunt Kitty went all out for Henry's farewell dinner with fried chicken, succotash made with the last of the corn and Kentucky Wonder beans, buttermilk biscuits, and peach jam. Sadie made a peach pie, and Rusty and Marion took turns turning the crank of the ice-cream maker after supper.

"Can't have peach pie without vanilla ice cream," said Uncle George, as he took a turn on the crank.

It had been a perfect evening, except that it was the last time Faith would see Henry. It was their good-bye, and it hung over the festivities like an unwelcome visitor. Mama deliberately engaged the rest of the family in a game of gin rummy after the cobbler and ice cream were devoured, so Faith and Henry could finally have time alone together on the porch. They sat on the porch swing listening to the night symphony and gazing at the heavy orange moon as it rose overhead.

"I brought you something," said Henry, as he reached in his pocket.

He pulled out a little midnight blue velvet box from Boucher's Jewelry Store in Logan.

"Oh, Henry, I don't have anything for you."

"You're all I want," he said. Faith opened the box. Inside was a silver-link bracelet with a single charm attached.

"I hope you like it. I thought of putting a heart on it but when I saw this, I thought it was perfect."

Faith held it up in the moonlight close to her eyes so she could get a clear look at the fat little silver peach. Attached to the stem was a silver leaf. Something was engraved on the leaf but it was too dark to make it out.

"It says '1932,'" said Henry. "There wasn't room to put our names like I wanted."

"It's perfect," said Faith.

She brushed a tear from her eye, hoping Henry didn't notice that she was crying.

This is hard enough without a bunch of crying, thought Faith.

Henry reached out and took the bracelet and hooked it around her wrist.

"I'll never take it off," said Faith, as she fingered the little peach.

"Oh, yes, you will, but I intend to add another charm the next time we're together," said Henry.

Lights were going out inside, and Henry knew that was his cue to leave soon.

"I've got something I want to tell you, Faith, but you've got to promise not to tell a soul."

"Of course I won't."

She leaned in, curious.

"I was in the kitchen packing up the last of the pantry this morning and I found something." He paused.

"What?" said Faith.

"The other shoe."

Faith felt her stomach fly up to her throat as she gasped. "Oh, my gosh. Now you really must give the shoes over to the sheriff. This might free Sidney, it may be his only chance. What did you do?"

"I didn't do anything. I just stuck it in with the other one and put the pair in my duffel bag."

"You have to take them to the sheriff. I'll go with you or you can leave the shoes with me and I'll take them to the sheriff myself. It might free Sidney. You've got to," said Faith.

"It won't help him, Faith. Everyone knows he's going to be convicted. It's just the way it is," said Henry. His voice was quiet, and he sounded so defeated. He continued, "I confronted my father this afternoon. I showed him both shoes and demanded he tell me what really happened."

"So what did he say?" asked Faith.

"You have to promise me that you will never repeat what I am about to tell you," said Henry.

"I already said I wouldn't tell. You know you can trust me."

"OK. My father only told me the truth because I threatened to turn the shoes in. Finally, he told me what really happened.

"On the night Gloria died she was at a party at our house. There was a lot of drinking as usual, and my mother got into a terrible argument with Gloria. Apparently my dad finally admitted to my mom to having the affair with Gloria. There was some pushing and shoving, and Mother pushed Gloria into the fireplace mantel. She fell and her neck broke." Henry took a breath. "Everyone was in shock. The ladies took Mother up to her room, and the men who were there carried Gloria's body to the basement."

"I thought her neck was slit," said Faith.

"That's what happened next. The men all decided that my mother had suffered enough, and no one wanted her to have to explain how Gloria really died. She was already so humiliated. So Dr. Colridge cut Gloria's neck to make it look like a murder, one that would take the suspicion away from my mother. Everyone swore to secrecy."

"So where does Sidney come into this mess?" asked Faith.

"Sidney agreed to dump the body. That's why there was blood in the dog car. And once he said that he had slept with Gloria, too, and he had the list of sixteen men that had also had relations with her, he was doomed. The clan would surely lynch him. So Father convinced Sidney to take the rap in exchange for a life sentence and no one bothering his family. It really was the best anyone could do, Faith."

Faith felt the anger rise inside of her. There was too much injustice for her to bear. She was smoldering with anger at Henry, at his father, and at his mother, too. How could they have put Sidney in such a hopeless position? She was angry at the justice system and at the Klan and at half of Logan County. "Clearly most everyone in Logan is in on the deal from the judge on down," said Faith.

Henry shrugged in agreement.

"Let's not talk about it anymore. There's nothing else to be done. We all just have to live with it. I don't want the trial to ruin our last night together. I almost wish I hadn't said anything about finding the other shoe," said Henry.

This is all so unfair, Faith thought.

But she willed herself to let it go and laid her head on Henry's shoulder. She sat very still, not saying a thing, mainly to calm herself. They sat this way for some time.

"Henry, I'm just so sorry." she said in a small voice. She squeezed his hand one last time. "Let's not say good-bye."

"OK, see you later, Faith." Henry kissed her on the top of her head, tenderly holding her face in his hands.

As Henry walked slowly down the porch steps, Rusty hung out his bedroom window and shouted, "Hail, Thundering Herd!"

"Go Marshall!" Henry shouted back, pumping his fist.

THIRTY-FIVE

THE WEATHER CHANGED EARLY FRIDAY morning. Faith woke up before sunrise with an ear-shattering single clap of thunder. She began counting, "One one thousand, two one thousand, three . . ."

Before she finished, the bedroom lit up with a bright flash of lightning. It had to have come from less than three miles away, somewhere in the hills surrounding the sturdy blue home down here in the holler. Nell woke up with the sudden light.

"Are you awake, Faith?"

"Uh huh. The thunder woke me. It's really close."

"I can't believe that you leave tomorrow. I wish you could just stay here forever. Do you think your folks would consider moving back? I'm going to miss you so. It will be so boring without you and your family, I don't know how I will manage. I can't imagine not having you here to talk to. What if Walter and I fall in love, you won't be here to calm me down and keep me steady? You must come back and be my maid of honor."

Faith barged in before Nell could continue. Nell had said all these things at least once a day for the last week, and Faith had other things to talk about. She held up her wrist with the shiny new bracelet in front of Nell's face.

"Oh, my gosh. Why didn't you tell me?" said Nell.

Faith laughed and gave her cousin a knowing look.

"OK, you couldn't get a word in, I know. Tell me every detail," said Nell as she inspected the jewelry. "A peach, how perfect. Oh, and 1932 on the leaf. It's so romantic that I can hardly breathe," said Nell.

"Well, take a breath, and I'll tell you everything," laughed Faith.

Faith did share almost everything with her cousin, what Henry said, how he put the bracelet on her wrist, the promises they made, even Rusty's cheer, but she didn't tell Nell about the shoe. It was a secret that wasn't hers to tell. Faith knew that Henry would see his family off in just a couple of hours and then catch the 10:23 to Huntington soon after.

She had a pretty good idea that Henry would have the shoes in his duffel bag and would toss them when he got to Marshall. She was angry that Henry had to live with the terrible secret about his parents.

"It's so sticky that I can't stay in this bed much longer," said Faith. "I'm going to go sit on the porch and listen to the birds one last time before we have to start the day. I know Aunt Kitty and Mama are going to have us all busy this morning getting everything ready for our party tonight. Thank goodness I've got my stuff mostly packed up and ready to go."

Papa was already sitting in one of the porch rocking chairs with a steaming cup of coffee in his hand.

"Guess the thunder woke you up, too. Want some coffee?" said Papa.

"I'll get some later, maybe. I'm afraid it will make me even hotter, if that's possible," said Faith. "Right now I just want to hear the birds one last time."

Charles smiled at his oldest child and said nothing. They rocked and listened. The early morning sky was steely pink against the thick clouds, and a few of the leaves that were rustling last night had begun to fall on the sidewalk on the other side of the front-yard fence. It was going to be a very hot, very muggy day.

"Aunt Kitty's got a list a mile long for me for tonight's party. She wants me to string lights across the porch, get ice for the drinks, and set up the sawhorses and plywood for tables, for a start. Those two sisters are planning on serving casts of thousands tonight." Charles took a drink of coffee and smiled. "George is probably counting his lucky stars that he has to work today. I expect you and Nell will be roped into the cooking this morning."

"When are you going into Logan for the trial today?" asked Faith.

"I'm not. The jury is still out, so it's just a matter of waiting for the verdict."

"Seems a shame, Papa. You haven't missed a day, and today's the day the verdict is supposed to come down."

"It's OK, and besides, I've been thinking. I know how much this trial has meant to you, being Henry's father is involved in the bloody mess. Kitty has me driving into Logan this afternoon to pick up Elizabeth and Cecelia. She wants them here to help with the setup. I'm thinking if we get done with Kitty's list in time, maybe I can leave a little early and swing by the courthouse for the verdict. Would you and Nell like to ride in with me?"

"Oh, Papa, do you mean it?" Faith got up, hugged her father, and planted a kiss on his bald spot.

The kitchen was a chaotic whirlwind, and Faith was glad to be part of it, despite the heat. It would take her mind off of Henry leaving this morning.

Bacon sizzled on the stove, and the greens were soaking in a big washtub, both needed for the wilted lettuce salad Kitty would put together just before the guests sat down to eat. Faith loved the sharp smell of apple cider vinegar and the sound of the hot bacon grease sputtering as it was poured over the lettuce and sliced onions. Uncle George said it was the only food that he could think of that sounded as good as it tasted. He was right.

Water boiled for the macaroni, and the potatoes were already cooling, each sister taking on one of the salads. Besides the three salads, a big pot of beans was baking slowly in the oven along with a fine country ham. Elizabeth promised to bring three pans of her peach cobbler.

Rusty and Marion were running in and out of the kitchen, Kitty was barking orders at Charles, and Mama was laughing about something with Nell.

This is another of those memories to freeze and keep, thought Faith.

She stood at the counter slicing pickles and tried hard to capture the moment. She had grown to love these moments, even in this miserable heat, and wondered how she could leave this family, this kitchen, this house, this place.

And yet, she missed her old life, the soft marine air, the parrot and the dog, her friends. She was anxious to complete her senior year at Broadway High School and then enroll at the University of Washington and get on with her life. She felt old, ready for so much more than working at Broadway Lunch and editing the school newspaper. She didn't know what was ahead, but Faith was certain it would be very different than what she had imagined for herself just three months ago when she stepped onto the train at King Street Station with her family.

The food was ready and the kitchen clean by noon. It was a good thing because the temperature outside must have been 95 degrees and inside it felt ten degrees hotter.

"You two better skedattle. You've got twenty minutes to clean up and be back down here. I'm leaving for Logan by 12:30," said Charles to Nell and Faith.

They threw off their aprons and ran upstairs to brush their hair, put on some lipstick, and get their hats.

"Hurry up, Faith. I don't want to give Uncle Charles any time to change his mind. I still can't believe that he's letting us go with him."

Faith, Nell, and Charles endured the crowded courthouse steps and the oppressive heat for two hours. Faith's feet were killing her, and her hair was a frizzled tangle from the humidity.

"I'm going to look a mess for my own party," she said to Nell at one point.

Charles was standing on a step below Nell and Faith. He pointed to his wristwatch. "I think we'd better leave. I promised Elizabeth I'd pick her up by 3:30 and it's three o'clock now," said Charles.

"Just ten more minutes, please, Papa," said Faith.

"Just ten minutes, then we've got to go."

"I think I'm going to wear my pink-eyelet sundress tonight, Faith. Do you think it looks too old-fashioned? Walter will be there and I so want to look good. What are you going to wear? I wouldn't wear the blue gingham dress, you'll be way too . . ."

"Shhh, here comes Bart Strout. They must have a verdict," interrupted Faith.

Bart stood on a wooden crate at the top of the wide courthouse stairs. There had to be at least a thousand people crowded on the steps and the courthouse yard below. The constant hum of the crowd began to quiet as folks spotted Bart.

"Quiet, everyone," shouted Bart. "We've got a verdict."

The throng gradually stopped talking. Faith crossed her fingers behind her back and forgot to breathe. Bart spoke.

"Sidney Williams has been found guilty on all charges."

The newspaperman's words hung heavy in the thick hot air. Faith was stunned despite what Henry had told her the night before. She had held out hope that justice would prevail in the end.

There was complete silence on the steps, and then one person began to clap. Faith would never forget that sound. That single clap was so loud, so clear. And then it grew like a wave reaching shore. People began to cheer and holler.

"I told you so."

"I knew they'd get that nigger."

"Praise the Lord. String him up."

She could actually feel the hateful words in her throat, taste a metallic bitterness in her mouth. She wanted to go home.

Papa reached up and took Faith's hand.

"Come on, Sweet Pea, it's time to go," said Papa.

She was crying. She couldn't help herself. She didn't even try to hide it. Tears flowed for Sidney, for the injustice that spilled over him. But the tears were also because she was leaving Peach Creek and all the people she had grown to love.

She was crying because her first love was gone and she didn't know if she would ever see him again. The tears were for the realization that life was really unfair. She cried for the girl she no longer was, and for the girl she had turned into this glorious messy summer, this summer in Peach Creek, West Virginia. Faith slowly walked down the courthouse steps with arms linked to Papa on one side and Nell on the other. She didn't look back.

* * *

ACKNOWLEDGMENTS

I AM GRATEFUL TO MY WRITING teachers, Sister Miriam Anna, Devon Jackson, and Steve Lorton, who guided me and gave me the confidence to continue to write. To my fellow writers Moses Howard for his wise counsel and Falaah Jones for getting the women of Peach Creek out of the kitchen. To Mary Ann Wiley for generously sharing her stories of growing up in Charleston, West Virginia. To Joanne Scaggs, my first Logan County friend. And to my family and friends who wouldn't let me throw in the towel.

Thanks also to the staff at the West Virginia Historical Museum and Archives, to Wedgwood's Top Pot Donuts where the first draft took form, and to F. Keith Davis, who wrote *The Secret Lies and Brutal Death of Mamie Thurman—a True Story.*

And to my publishing team for their expertise, patience and generosity: Annie Pearson, book designer and project manager; Temre Stanchfield and Nancy Stanchfield, cover artists; Willo Bellwood, graphic designer; Cynthia White, copy editor; and David Leder, Web designer.

And to my lovely daughters who are always there for me.

Finally, a loving thank you to my mother, Dorothy Ward Malo, for writing the journal *Travels of a Jack-Ass* that sparked the idea for *A Summer in Peach Creek.*

ABOUT THE AUTHOR

A SEATTLE NATIVE, MICHELE MALO lives in the city with her dog, Mario. She loves gardens and travel and hanging out with her grandchildren.

This is her first novel.

Made in the USA
Charleston, SC
08 June 2015